MURDER IN DUBLIN

HAZEL CHASE MYSTERIES
BOOK 3

ARTHUR PEARCE

Copyright © 2025 Arthur Pearce

All rights reserved.

No part of this book may be reproduced, distributed, or transmitted in any form or by any means, including photocopying, recording, or other electronic or mechanical methods, without the prior written permission of the author, except in the case of brief quotations embodied in critical reviews and certain other noncommercial uses permitted by copyright law. For permission requests, please contact the author.

"Murder in Dublin" is a work of fiction. Names, characters, businesses, places, events and incidents either are products of the author's imagination or are used fictitiously. Any resemblance to actual persons, living or dead, events, or locales is entirely coincidental.

ISBN: 979-8-2746-3564-6

1

The drizzle hit Hazel's face the moment she stepped off the plane onto the mobile stairs. Dublin's welcome gift, apparently. She hunched her shoulders against the unexpected chill, her thin cardigan about as useful as tissue paper. The temperature was cold enough to make her shiver—a far cry from Rome's September heat that had left her sweating through every shirt she owned.

    She hurried down the stairs, joining the stream of passengers making their way across the wet pavement toward the terminal. Her California-conditioned body protested the chill with immediate goosebumps. The wind cut through her clothes like it had a personal vendetta against tourists who didn't check weather forecasts.

Why hadn't she looked up Dublin's climate? Because she'd been too busy researching Professor Murphy's published papers and trying to understand terms like "biomolecular synthesis" and "pharmaceutical compound isolation." Like that would help if she froze to death before meeting him.

The terminal building beckoned with its promise of warmth. Hazel picked up her pace, weaving through the crowd of passengers. Inside, the temperature difference was immediate and welcome. She followed the signs for passport control, her sneakers squeaking on the polished floor.

The walk stretched longer than expected through a corridor lined with advertisements and historical displays. Her mind drifted to Rome, to Giorgio's apartment just two weeks ago. Another murder solved. Another revenge plot uncovered. Was this her life now? Flying around Europe, stumbling into other people's revenge plots while chasing her own family mysteries?

She'd started this journey to learn new pastry techniques in Paris, not to become some kind of international amateur detective. But here she was, heading to meet yet another person from her parents' past, hoping this time she'd get answers without anyone dying in the process.

Though given Professor Murphy's age—seventy-five according to Trinity's faculty page—she should probably hurry. The way her luck had been running, he'd keel over from a heart attack right as she introduced herself. "Hi, I'm Hazel Chase, here to ask about my parents, and—oh, are you okay? No? Dead? Great."

The passport control queue moved quickly. Green signs directed EU and UK citizens to one line, everyone else to another. When Hazel reached the booth, the officer—a woman with bright red hair pulled back in a neat bun and laugh lines around her eyes—greeted her with a smile that seemed genuinely warm rather than professionally mandated.

"Welcome to Ireland! First time?"

"Yes, first time." Hazel handed over her passport.

"Brilliant! How long will you be staying?"

"Just a few days."

"Ah, that's hardly enough to see Dublin, let alone the rest of Ireland." The officer stamped the passport with practiced ease. "What brings you to our fair city? Business or pleasure?"

"Pleasure. Sightseeing." The lie came easily now. She'd had plenty of practice in Paris and Rome.

"Well, you picked a grand time for it. September's lovely—when it's not raining, which is about half the time." The officer leaned forward conspiratorially, her voice dropping as if sharing state secrets. "If you get a chance, take the DART out to Howth. Beautiful coastal walk, best fish and chips in Ireland. And Temple Bar's touristy but worth one visit for the atmosphere. Just don't buy drinks there unless you want to mortgage your house."

"Thanks, I'll keep that in mind."

"Oh, and if you're into history, Kilmainham Gaol is fascinating. Bit grim, being a former prison and all, but important to Irish history." The officer handed back the passport. "Enjoy your stay!"

Hazel walked away thinking that French and Italian immigration had been all business—stamp, next, move along. The Irish officer had been like chatting with a helpful aunt who actually wanted you to enjoy her country. Maybe this was an Irish thing, this immediate friendliness. Or maybe she'd just gotten lucky.

Her phone buzzed as she waited at baggage claim, watching the same three suitcases circle endlessly like they were showing off. International roaming had kicked in, and there was already a text from Janet.

Found any cute Irish guys yet?

Hazel checked the time. It would be about 5 AM in California. Had Janet even slept? They'd talked three hours ago before Hazel's flight.

She typed back: *Just landed. Go to sleep. Only Irish guy I'm meeting is 75-year-old professor.*

The response came immediately: *Age is just a number. Maybe he's a silver fox. Distinguished academic type.*

Janet. Sleep. Now.

Fine. But if you meet any younger versions, I call dibs on photos.

Hazel shook her head, pocketing the phone as her suitcase appeared on the carousel. Janet's ability to function on no sleep while maintaining her questionable sense of humor defied medical science.

Outside, the drizzle had given way to actual sunshine. Irish weather apparently had commitment issues. Hazel spotted a taxi near the exit, its driver—a stereotypically Irish-looking man with reddish hair and ruddy cheeks—helping a family unload their mountain of bags from the trunk.

"Can you take me to city center?" Hazel asked as he handed the last suitcase to the father. "I've got a B&B booked near Trinity College."

"Course I can, love. Let me get your bag there." He hefted her suitcase into the trunk with surprising ease, whistling something that might have been a traditional Irish tune. "Go on, hop in."

Hazel walked to the right side of the car, reached for the door handle, and froze. The steering wheel stared back at her through the window, mocking her American assumptions.

Right. Ireland. They drove on the left here.

Her hesitation lasted just long enough for the driver to notice. He closed the trunk and grinned, his whole face crinkling with amusement. "Want to drive, do you? I mean, I'm knackered from the early start, so if you're offering..."

"Sorry." Heat crept up Hazel's neck as she walked around to the left side. "Still getting used to the whole wrong-side thing. I mean, not wrong for you, obviously. Just different."

"Ah, you're grand. Happens all the time with the Yanks." He slid into the driver's seat as she settled in the back. The taxi smelled faintly of air freshener trying to mask decades of passengers. "Though I did have one fella last month who tried to get in the driver's side three times before his wife physically dragged him to the other door. Then he spent the whole ride gripping the handle like I was driving on the wrong side. You're doing better than him."

Great. At least she wasn't the worst American tourist he'd encountered. Small victories.

2

The taxi pulled away from the airport, and the driver glanced at her in the rearview mirror, his eyes crinkled with perpetual good humor. He said something that included the word "States" but the rest was lost in what sounded like Gaelic mixed with English. His accent had thickened considerably from their brief exchange outside, or maybe she just hadn't been paying attention before.

"Sorry?"

"Where in America?" He spoke slower, but somehow that made it worse, like listening to a record played at the wrong speed.

"Oh! California. Small town called Fillmore."

"Cali-forn-ya!" He dragged out the syllables with obvious delight. "Sunshine and film stars, eh? Bit different from this." He gestured at the sky, which had decided to demonstrate Irish weather's full range by producing rain from nowhere. Drops splattered the windshield in an irregular rhythm, like nature's morse code.

"We have our share of rain too," Hazel said, though Fillmore's occasional drizzle hardly compared to whatever meteorological mood swing was happening outside the taxi window.

He said something else that might have been about rain or trains or possibly Spain. Hazel caught maybe every third word, her brain working overtime to decode the accent. Something about "grand altogether" and what sounded like "your man there now."

"Mm-hmm," she said, hoping that was an appropriate response.

"Ah, so you've been there too?" He sounded pleased, turning slightly in his seat to glance at her.

Shit. Been where? What had she just agreed to?

"Well, not exactly…" she hedged.

"No? But you just said you had." Now he sounded confused. "Fair play to you if you haven't though, it's a long way to go just for the craic."

"I thought you asked if I liked the rain?"

He burst out laughing, a sound that needed no translation. "Jaysus, no! I asked if you'd been to Spain. On account of the rain, you know—'the rain in Spain falls mainly on the plain' and all that."

"Oh." Hazel laughed too, partly from embarrassment and partly from relief. "Sorry, I'm still adjusting to the accent."

"Ah, you're alright. I'm from the Midlands, we've got a particular way of talking. Different from the Dubs, different from Cork, definitely different from the North. My own mother swears we sound like we're chewing rocks half the time. Ireland's got more accents per square mile than anywhere else, I reckon."

Multiple Irish accents. Of course. Because understanding one wasn't challenging enough. Hazel had thought Ireland would be easier to navigate than France or Italy—everyone spoke English, right? She hadn't factored in the part where the English might as well be a foreign language.

"How many accents are we talking about?"

"Oh, loads. You could drive an hour in any direction and find people talking completely different. My own mother struggles with my wife's family's accent, and they're only from Sligo."

The taxi merged onto a highway—motorway, Hazel corrected herself, trying to think in Irish terms. The driver kept up a steady stream of commentary, and gradually, miraculously, her ears began to adjust. Patterns emerged in his speech, the rhythm of dropped consonants and musical vowels becoming almost predictable.

"First time in Dublin?" he asked, and this time she caught it perfectly.

"First time in Ireland, actually."

"Ah, brilliant! You'll love it. Friendliest country in the world, though I might be biased." He glanced at her in the mirror again. "What's the plan then? Bit of sightseeing?"

"Exactly. Trinity College, Temple Bar, the usual tourist things." The half-truth felt comfortable now, like a worn jacket.

"Good on you. Though Temple Bar's a rip-off, just so you know. Ten euros for a pint! Daylight robbery. You want a proper pub, try someplace off the beaten track."

"Any recommendations?"

"Depends what you're after. Traditional music? Good conversation? Cheap drinks?" He considered. "Actually, you know what you should see? Ireland's oldest pub. Not in Dublin, mind—it's out in Athlone, where I'm from. Sean's Bar, been serving drinks since the year 900."

"Did you say 900? As in over a thousand years ago?"

"That's the one! Though between you and me, I reckon they've replaced a few things since then. But the tavern's been there right enough. Survived Vikings, Cromwell, the British, and worst of all, stag parties from England." He chuckled at his own joke. "My name's Sean too, actually." He pointed at his taxi license displayed on the dashboard. "Though not that old, before you ask."

Hazel leaned forward to read the license.

"It's pronounced 'Shawn,'" he said with exaggerated clarity. "You Yanks always want to say 'Seen' like you've spotted something."

"I was going to say 'Shawn,'" Hazel protested, though she absolutely had been about to say "Seen."

"Course you were." His grin in the mirror suggested he wasn't buying it. "Though you wouldn't be the first. Had an American last year who kept calling me 'See-an' the whole ride. Poor fella was from Texas, kept apologizing in that big drawl of his. 'Sorry, See-an, I just can't get my mouth around it.' I didn't have the heart to correct him after the fifth time."

The weather continued its theatrical performance outside. Sun gave way to sheets of rain that turned the windshield into a waterfall, which transformed into a light mist that made everything look like an impressionist painting, then back to sun, all accompanied by wind that seemed determined to blow pedestrians into traffic. Hazel watched a woman's umbrella turn inside out, reform itself, then give up entirely, its metal ribs pointing in directions that defied physics.

"Is the weather always this... indecisive?"

Sean laughed. "This? This is calm. You should see it when it's really putting on a show. Had a day last week where we got sun, rain, hail, and fog in the space of an hour. The weather forecast just showed a picture of a confused sheep." He flicked the windshield wipers to a faster setting. "We say if you don't like the weather in Ireland, wait five minutes. Though sometimes that's optimistic—might take ten."

Buildings grew denser as they approached the city center. Georgian townhouses lined the streets, their doors—red, blue, yellow, green, purple—adding splashes of color to the gray day. Or sunny day. Or rainy day. The weather hadn't decided yet. Brass plaques beside many doors announced solicitors, accountants, and other businesses.

"See the colored doors?" Sean gestured unnecessarily—they were impossible to miss. "Back in the day, when Queen Victoria died, the Brits wanted everyone to paint their doors black for mourning. The Irish, being contrary sorts, painted them every color but black. Been that way ever since."

"Is that true?"

"Might be. Might not be. But it's a good story, and that's what matters." He navigated around a double-decker bus that was attempting to occupy two lanes simultaneously. "My wife's always on at me to move somewhere predictable," Sean continued. "Spain or somewhere. Guarantee of sunshine, beaches, all that. But where's the fun in that? Knowing what you're going to get every day?" He shook his head. "Give me four seasons in one afternoon any day. Keeps you on your toes."

"I can see the appeal," Hazel said, though privately she thought consistent weather had its merits. Like knowing whether to pack a sundress or a parka. Or both. Probably both in Ireland.

"Plus, the tourists love it. 'Oh, we experienced all of Irish weather in one day!' they say, like they've won a prize." He slowed for a red light, drumming his fingers on the steering wheel. "Mind you, they're less enthusiastic when they're soaked through, but that's what pubs are for."

"Here we are then." Sean pulled up outside a narrow townhouse with a small sign reading *The Liffey Rose B&B*. The building was painted a cheerful yellow that somehow managed to look sunny even under gray skies. Lace curtains in the windows gave it a homey appearance, and window boxes overflowed with flowers that had apparently made peace with Irish weather. "You picked a good spot. Walking distance to everything, great location for the city center. Most B&Bs around here do a proper full Irish breakfast—just pace yourself with the black pudding. Americans always underestimate it."

"Black pudding?"

"Best not to ask what's in it. Just eat it and thank me later." He got out to retrieve her suitcase from the trunk. "That'll be thirty-two euros, love."

Hazel paid, adding a tip that made Sean's eyebrows rise appreciatively.

"Ah, you're very good. Best of luck to you now." He handed her a business card that had seen better days, the edges soft from living in his pocket. "If you need a ride anywhere, give us a shout. I'll give you the scenic route, throw in some history lessons free of charge. Some of them might even be true."

"Thanks, Sean. For the ride and the advice."

"Not a bother. Enjoy Dublin. Don't let the weather scare you off—just dress like you're expecting everything at once."

As his taxi pulled away, Hazel stood on the sidewalk with her suitcase, looking up at the B&B. The sun chose that moment to disappear again, replaced by what could only be described as aggressive mist—not quite rain but definitely not not-rain. She grabbed her suitcase and hurried inside before the weather could change its mind again.

She was definitely going to need all the luck Sean had wished her.

3

The B&B's entrance hall was cramped but warm, with floral wallpaper that had probably been there since the seventies and a smell of furniture polish mixed with something baking. A small table held brochures for local attractions, and a grandfather clock ticked heavily in the corner. A woman emerged from what Hazel assumed was the kitchen, wiping her hands on an apron decorated with shamrocks that had been embroidered with more enthusiasm than skill.

"You must be Hazel! I'm Mrs. O'Neill. Welcome, welcome!" She was exactly what Hazel had pictured when booking a Dublin B&B—mid-sixties, gray hair in soft curls, smile lines that suggested a lifetime of hospitality, and the kind of complexion that spoke of

Irish mists and strong tea. "Did you have a good flight? Not too bumpy, I hope? September can be rough with the winds."

"It was fine, thank you."

"Oh, American! How lovely. Whereabouts? No, wait, let me guess." She tilted her head, studying Hazel like she was a puzzle to solve. "Not East Coast, you don't have the accent. Not Southern either. California?"

"Good guess."

"I watch a lot of American television," Mrs. O'Neill admitted with a laugh. "CSI, Law and Order, all those shows where everyone's either a cop or a criminal. We get a lot of Americans this time of year. Less crowded than summer, better prices." She bustled behind a small desk that served as reception, its surface covered with papers, keys, and a ceramic leprechaun that looked vaguely threatening. "Now, you're with us for four nights, is that right?"

"That's right."

"Perfect. You've got room three, lovely view of the garden. Well, I say garden—it's more of a courtyard with notions. But the roses are doing well this year." She produced an actual key, not a key card, attached to a wooden fob with the number 3 burned into it. "Breakfast is between seven and nine-thirty. Full Irish, continental, or I can do porridge if you prefer. Though between you and me, you haven't lived until you've tried my black pudding. Won an award at the county fair three years running."

The second black pudding recommendation of the day. Hazel was starting to think it was some kind of Dublin conspiracy.

"Now, you're perfectly placed here," Mrs. O'Neill continued, pulling out a well-worn map that had been folded and refolded so many times the creases were wearing through. "Trinity College is just there, five minutes' walk. Temple Bar's about ten minutes that way—though mind yourself at night, gets a bit rowdy. Grafton

Street for shopping, St. Stephen's Green if you want a nice walk. Oh, and the Book of Kells at Trinity, you have to see that, though book early or the tickets sell out."

She continued marking the map with X's and circles, creating what looked like a tourist's treasure map. Her handwriting was tiny and precise, adding notes like "good coffee here" and "tourist trap – avoid!"

"Any questions, love?"

"No, this is perfect. Thank you."

"Grand. Your room's just up these stairs, second door on the right. There's tea and biscuits in the room, and if you need anything at all, just give a shout. I'm usually pottering around somewhere."

The stairs creaked with every step, the sound of a house that had settled into itself over decades. Faded photographs lined the stairway walls—Dublin through the years, from horse-drawn carriages to modern trams. Room three was small but clean, with a double bed covered in a quilted bedspread featuring Celtic knots, a wooden wardrobe that looked like it could tell stories, and a window overlooking a courtyard where roses were indeed doing well against all meteorological odds.

Hazel set her suitcase by the wardrobe and sat on the bed, testing the mattress. Firm but not uncomfortable. The whole room felt like staying at a grandmother's house—if her grandmother had been Irish and substantially less paranoid than Bridget.

She unpacked a few essentials, hanging up the jacket she should have worn on the plane. The room came equipped with an electric kettle, proper teacups with tiny shamrocks painted on them, and a selection of tea bags that suggested Mrs. O'Neill took her hospitality seriously. Earl Grey, Irish Breakfast, something called Barry's Tea that seemed important based on its prominent placement, and mysteriously, one lonely bag of Lipton that looked like it had been exiled to the back of the basket.

But the tea could wait, Hazel couldn't sit still. Trinity College was just five minutes away. She'd emailed Professor Murphy two days ago but hadn't gotten a reply—not surprising with the new term starting tomorrow. She'd just have to show up at the Trinity Biomedical Sciences Institute and hope to catch him.

For now, though, the campus was open to the public. She could walk where her parents had walked, see what they'd seen. The pull was irresistible.

She grabbed her jacket—learning from her airport experience—and headed back downstairs. Mrs. O'Neill had disappeared, though the sound of a vacuum cleaner suggested she was attacking dust somewhere in the building's depths. The grandfather clock chimed the half hour as Hazel passed.

Outside, the weather had settled on overcast with a chance of everything. Hazel turned left, following Mrs. O'Neill's directions toward Trinity. The sidewalks were narrower than she expected, forcing pedestrians into an elaborate dance of dodging and weaving. Shop windows displayed everything from traditional woolens to modern electronics, the old and new pressed together like they'd been forced to share a small apartment.

A bus roared past, startling her with its proximity. She'd stepped too close to the curb, forgetting that traffic came from the opposite direction. A woman walking behind her made a tutting sound that transcended cultural boundaries—the universal noise of "tourist almost getting herself killed."

She paid more attention after that, looking right before crossing instead of left, though her American instincts fought her every step. By the time she reached the second intersection, she'd developed a system: look both ways twice, then once more for good measure. Paranoid, but better than becoming Dublin's latest traffic statistic.

The entrance to Trinity appeared ahead, an archway cut into a long stone building that looked like it had been guarding the college for centuries. A security guard stood to one side, observing the flow of people with professional boredom. Students streamed in and out, backpacks and messenger bags marking them as clearly as uniforms would have. Some tourists mingled among them, cameras at the ready, but the late afternoon timing meant the crowds were manageable.

Hazel passed through the archway and stopped.

4

The courtyard that opened before her was massive, a green rectangle surrounded by stone buildings that belonged in a period drama. But it was the bell tower that drew her eye—the Campanile, rising from the center of the square. She'd seen it in photos, of course, but photos couldn't capture the sense of age, of thousands of students over hundreds of years passing beneath its shadow.

She walked toward it slowly, trying to imagine her parents here as students. Twenty-somethings with their whole lives ahead of them, no idea that they'd die in a car accident before their daughter could form proper memories of them. Had they walked this same path? Sat on the grass where students now sprawled with books? Made plans for a future that would be cut brutally short?

Her phone held the photo she'd found in Charles Lambert's office—Charles, Vittoria Rossi, and her parents standing somewhere on this campus, young and grinning like they owned the world. The original was safe in her suitcase, too precious to carry around Dublin's unpredictable weather.

She studied the photo, then looked around. The Campanile was prominent, but it wasn't in their picture. The buildings looked familiar but not quite right. Where had they been standing?

Hazel turned in a slow circle, comparing angles, trying to match the historic architecture to her parents' old photo. Students passed her, probably wondering why the tourist was spinning in place like a confused compass. Then she turned back toward the entrance and felt her breath catch.

There. The building with the archway she'd just walked through, the clock centered above it on the building's facade. The same clock that appeared in the background of her parents' photo, frozen at a different time but otherwise unchanged.

She walked back toward the entrance, positioning herself where the photographer must have stood. Her parents had been here. Right here. Her mother laughing at something. Her father's arm casually around her shoulders. Charles making some theatrical gesture. Vittoria trying to look serious but smiling despite herself.

The present overlapped with the past, and for a moment Hazel could almost see them. Four students who'd become friends over cheap beer and bad music, who'd spent late nights studying and early mornings regretting their choices. Who'd had no idea that three decades later, Charles would be murdered in Paris, Vittoria would hide from mysterious men in Rome, and Thomas and Olivia's orphaned daughter would be standing here, trying to piece together their secrets.

"Excuse me, are you alright?"

Hazel startled. An Indian student stood nearby, concern written across her face. She wore a Trinity hoodie and carried a backpack that looked heavy enough to contain a small library. Hazel realized she'd been standing in the same spot for who knew how long, staring at nothing.

"Yes, sorry. I was just—" She held up her phone. "Would you mind taking a photo of me? With that building behind me—the one with the clock?"

"Of course!" The student's concern morphed into a smile. She took Hazel's phone. "Is this your first time at Trinity?"

"First time in Dublin, actually."

"Oh, how exciting! I'm in my third year, still get lost sometimes. The campus is bigger than it looks." She lined up the shot. "Okay, ready? Maybe step a little to your left... perfect!"

She took several photos, angling for the best light. "There you go. The front arch is everyone's favorite backdrop. Though personally, I prefer the Long Room Library. Have you seen it yet?"

"Not yet. Maybe tomorrow."

"Definitely worth it. They charge admission, but it's like stepping into Harry Potter. Or Beauty and the Beast, if you prefer Disney to wizards." The student handed back the phone. "Fair warning though—no flash photography allowed inside, and they're strict about it. Security guards watch like hawks. Enjoy your visit!"

She hurried off, probably late for something, leaving Hazel alone with her ghosts again. She looked at the photos the student had taken. Same building, same clock, same spot where her parents had stood. But now it was her, thirty years later, trying to understand the life they'd lived and the secrets they'd left behind.

The resemblance to her mother was undeniable in this light. Same dark hair, same way of holding her shoulders, same curve to her smile. Genetics were strange—all those possibilities narrowing down to create a daughter who looked like an echo of someone she barely remembered.

A tour group passed by, led by a student walking backwards with impressive confidence, gesturing at buildings and rattling off dates. "And the Campanile there was built in 1853, standing at 98 feet tall. Legend says if you walk under it as a student, you'll fail your exams, so you'll see everyone taking the long way around during finals..."

"Okay," Hazel said quietly, not caring if passing students thought she was talking to herself. "Enough emotional archaeology for one day."

Tomorrow she'd try to find Professor Murphy and maybe finally get answers about her parents' research, their money, their death. Or maybe she'd just find more questions. Either way, she needed to be ready, not standing here getting weepy over old photos.

She had the whole afternoon ahead of her. Dublin waited beyond Trinity's walls—pubs and history and probably more weather changes than she could count. She should explore, get a feel for the city, maybe find dinner somewhere that didn't involve black pudding.

As long as she didn't stumble over any bodies along the way.

She'd had enough of murder for one month. For one lifetime, really. Dublin could keep its mysteries to itself—she was only here for her parents' secrets, nothing more.

Though with her luck, she'd probably find a corpse in her breakfast tomorrow.

Hazel shook off the morbid thought and headed back through the archway, out into the city streets. Whatever Dublin had in store for her, at least it couldn't be worse than being locked in a room with murderers.

Famous last thoughts.

5

Hazel's feet found their rhythm on Dublin's sidewalks as she headed toward the river. The gray sky held steady for once, neither threatening rain nor promising sun—just existing in that Irish limbo Sean had warned her about. She'd take it. After the Roman heat that had left her perpetually sticky, this cool September air felt like a gift.

The streets grew busier as she approached what had to be the River Liffey. More tourists appeared, phones out for photos, consulting Google Maps like digital lifelines against getting lost. She crossed with a crowd at the traffic light, remembering to look right first, then left, then right again because paranoia had served her well so far.

That's when she saw it.

Rising above the buildings ahead, a metallic needle pierced the sky. The thing had to be two or three times taller than anything around it, catching what little light filtered through the clouds and throwing it back defiantly. It looked like someone had dropped a piece of modern art into the middle of historic Dublin and forgotten to pick it up.

Perfect weather for a walk, she decided. Might as well check out the giant needle while the sky held its truce.

The bridge she crossed buzzed with activity—double-decker buses rumbling past, cars navigating between pedestrians who stopped mid-span for photos despite the traffic. Locals wove through it all with practiced ease while tourists clustered at the edges, cameras ready. Hazel pulled out her phone and opened Google Maps, curious where exactly she'd wandered.

O'Connell Bridge, apparently. And that monument ahead with the statues? O'Connell Monument. The wide street stretching beyond it? O'Connell Street.

This O'Connell guy must have been Ireland's answer to George Washington, she thought. Mental note: look him up later.

A cluster of people near the monument caught her attention. A tour guide held a small flag aloft—emerald green, naturally—and gestured enthusiastically at the statues. Hazel drifted closer, hovering at the back of the group. The last time she'd joined a tour group in Rome, someone had ended up dead. But surely lightning wouldn't strike twice. Or in her case, three times.

"Daniel O'Connell," the guide was saying, his accent thick but understandable, "known as The Liberator. Fought for Catholic emancipation in the 1820s without spilling a drop of blood. The man could rally crowds of hundreds of thousands with just his voice—no microphones back then, mind you."

The guide pointed to the monument's base. "Those bullet holes you see? From the 1916 Easter Rising. The rebels used the statue for cover while fighting the British. Poor Daniel took more damage dead than he ever did alive."

Someone in the group raised a camera, and the guide waited patiently for the photo before continuing. "Now, if you'll follow me, we'll head up to see Dublin's most controversial landmark—the Spire."

The group moved forward like a multicultural centipede, and Hazel let herself be swept along. Why not? She was already exploring the city—might as well learn something from a professional guide instead of wandering aimlessly.

O'Connell Street pulsed with life. Shop fronts competed for attention— Foot Locker, Subway, McDonald's wedged between local businesses like a familiar face in a foreign crowd. Street performers worked their pitches, a living statue here, a guitarist there, someone doing something athletic with a soccer ball that defied physics. The smell of grease from a nearby burger joint mixed with exhaust fumes and the occasional whiff of perfume from passing shoppers.

"The Spire of Dublin," the guide announced as they approached the needle, "officially called the Monument of Light. One hundred and twenty-one meters tall—that's about four hundred feet for our American friends. Erected in 2003 where Nelson's Pillar used to stand before the IRA blew it up in 1966."

Hazel craned her neck to follow the monument's line skyward. Up close, it was even more impressive, its stainless steel surface reflecting the city in warped fragments. The base was wider than she'd expected, tapering to a point so fine it seemed to disappear into the clouds.

"Locals have more colorful names for it," the guide continued with a grin. "The Stiletto in the Ghetto, the Nail in the Pale, the Pin in the Bin. Dubliners love their rhyming slang almost as much as they love complaining about modern architecture."

The group chuckled and dispersed slightly for photos. Hazel pulled out her phone, framing the Spire against the moody sky. She started to post it to her Stories, then hesitated. Francesco Moretti had found her in Rome through social media, showing up at tourist sites, restaurants, wherever she went with suspicious timing. Better to post later, when she was somewhere else entirely. Who knew if someone else like Francesco was waiting for her to broadcast her location? She wasn't making that mistake again.

She attempted a selfie, angling the phone up from below to capture both her face and the Spire's full height. The resulting photo made her chin look like it was plotting world domination. Delete. Try again from a different angle. Still terrible. Some monuments weren't meant for selfies.

Movement to her right caught her attention. A crowd had gathered around what looked like a massive circular screen, maybe eight feet across, installed on a sturdy square base. People pointed and waved at it, their faces animated with delight. Hazel checked both directions—twice—and crossed the street to investigate.

The thing looked like something from a science fiction movie, all sleek metal and LED technology. On the screen, a public square filled with people waving enthusiastically at the camera. But waving at what?

6

A woman about Hazel's age stood nearby, grinning at the screen with the satisfaction of someone enjoying a private joke. She wore a navy Eason uniform polo and sensible flats that suggested a long day on her feet.

"Excuse me," Hazel ventured. "What is this?"

The woman turned, her accent clear despite its Dublin inflection. "First time seeing the Portal? It's brilliant, isn't it? Live feed from other cities around the world. I stop here on my way home from work—better than telly."

"Live feed? You mean those people are—"

"Waving at us right now, yeah. See the flag there?" She pointed to a small symbol at the top of the screen. "That's Vilnius, capital of Lithuania."

The Lithuanian crowd had grown, people of all ages making heart shapes with their hands. The Irish crowd responded in kind, creating a moment of connection across thousands of miles. Someone held up a baby, and the Lithuanians cooed visibly, their delight needing no translation.

"I'm terrible with flags," Hazel admitted as the screen flickered and changed. Geography had been her worst subject in school—she'd spent most of those classes doodling in her notebook while Mrs. Adams droned on about exports and capitals. Now she wished she'd paid more attention. "Where's this?"

"Poland—Lublin, specifically. Lovely people, the Poles. Watch this." The woman held up both hands in a heart shape, and several people on screen immediately reciprocated. Both crowds waved enthusiastically, a grandfather lifting a small child onto his shoulders for a better view, teenagers taking selfies with the portal in the background.

It was absurdly wholesome. No words exchanged, no language needed, just humans being pleased to see other humans existing somewhere else on the planet. Hazel found herself smiling.

"How many countries does it connect to?"

"Three at the moment. Lithuania, Poland, and—" The woman's expression shifted as the screen changed again. "Ah. America. Philadelphia, specifically."

The Stars and Stripes appeared at the top of the screen. Only a few people stood in view, but their body language was completely different. Instead of waves or hearts, they offered middle fingers and obscene gestures.

Heat crawled up Hazel's neck. Of course it was Americans acting like idiots. Every other country had managed sweet, sincere interactions, and her countrymen went straight for juvenile vulgarity.

The woman laughed. "With the Yanks, you never know what you'll get. Sometimes it's lovely families, other times..." She gestured at the screen where someone was now pretending to hump the camera. "Where are you from yourself? Canada? Your accent sounds North American."

"Canada, yes." The lie came instantly. "Vancouver."

"Lovely! I've a cousin in Toronto. Complete opposite side, I know, but still."

Hazel made appropriate Canadian noises and excused herself before the conversation could venture into specific neighborhoods or hockey teams. California, Canada—both started with "C." Close enough for tourist purposes.

Dark clouds had muscled their way across the sky while she'd been watching the Portal, looking heavy with rain that hadn't quite committed to falling. Sean's prediction about five-minute weather changes was holding up. Time to head back before—

A drop hit her forehead. Then another. Then the sky gave up all pretense and released a proper drizzle.

Hazel pulled up Google Maps, searching for food options near her B&B. Her stomach had moved past polite suggestions into outright demands. The Bank on College Green popped up—high ratings, lots of reviews, and only a ten-minute walk. Perfect.

She set off at a brisk pace, the drizzle just heavy enough to be annoying but not quite warranting the umbrella she'd left in her room. Mental note: always carry an umbrella in Dublin. Also possibly a raincoat. And waterproof shoes. Maybe just wear scuba gear everywhere.

The streets grew more confusing as she navigated, trying to match the blue dot on her phone to actual reality. She stepped off a curb, looking left first—

A bell clanged frantically. A sleek tram bore down on her, the driver's expression suggesting he'd seen too many tourists attempt suicide by Luas. Hazel jumped back, heart hammering, as the tram whooshed past in a blur of green and silver.

Right. Trams. Those were a thing here.

When would she get used to left-side traffic? Probably about five minutes before leaving for the next city—if there was a next city. Maybe Professor Murphy would have all the answers and she could finally go home instead of continuing this European mystery tour.

The Bank on College Green appeared just as the drizzle decided to upgrade to actual rain. Hazel ducked inside, shaking water from her hair, and stopped short.

The interior belonged in a museum. Soaring ceilings decorated with elaborate plasterwork, columns that looked like they could hold up the sky, chandeliers that probably cost more than her car back home. The whole space screamed "former bank" in the most elegant way possible, all marble and mahogany and careful restoration.

"Table for one?" The hostess appeared at her elbow, professional smile in place.

"Yes, please."

"I'm afraid there's a bit of a wait—we're quite busy this time of day. Would you mind having a drink at the bar while a table frees up? Shouldn't be more than fifteen or twenty minutes."

Hazel's stomach lodged a formal protest. She wanted food, not drinks. But the woman's manner was so polite, and the interior so impressive, that refusing felt churlish.

"That's fine."

The hostess led her to an enormous bar that looked like it could serve half of Dublin on a busy night. Most stools were occupied, but Hazel spotted an empty one near a young couple and claimed it before someone else could.

"What can I get you?" The bartender materialized instantly, all efficiency and rolled sleeves.

"Just water for now, thanks."

He nodded and moved away. Hazel watched him work, not really paying attention to the couple beside her until certain words drifted over: Trinity, biochemistry, morning lecture...

"—cannot believe Murphy assigned reading before term even started," the young man was saying. He had the rangy build of someone who'd grown tall quickly and hadn't quite filled out yet, dark hair flopping into his eyes as he gestured with his pint. "Absolute sadist."

"You didn't do it, did you?" His companion, a woman with auburn hair and an amused expression, shook her head. "Patrick, he literally said it would help with tomorrow's lecture."

"Tomorrow's lecture is just introduction waffle. 'Welcome back, here's what we'll cover this term, don't forget to buy my textbook.' I've been to enough Murphy lectures to know the pattern."

Hazel's water arrived. She sipped it slowly, mind racing. Professor Murphy. Biochemistry. Trinity. What were the chances?

"At least he tells good stories," the woman continued. "Remember last term when he went off about that pharmaceutical company in Boston? Twenty minutes about patent law when we were supposed to be learning about enzyme inhibitors."

"Emily, he could tell stories about paint drying and make them interesting. Doesn't mean I did the reading."

This had to be the same Professor Murphy. How many biochemistry professors named Murphy could Trinity have? Hazel's plan to somehow track him down tomorrow was looking shakier by the minute—she'd been relying on luck and determination, neither of which had a great track record lately.

Time to take a chance.

7

"Excuse me," she said, turning slightly toward them. "I couldn't help overhearing—you mentioned Professor Murphy?"

They both looked at her, and Hazel braced for irritation at the interruption. Instead, the woman—Emily—smiled openly.

"Guilty of eavesdropping, are we? Yeah, Professor Cornelius Murphy. Do you know him?"

"Sort of. He taught my parents years ago. I'm actually in Dublin hoping to talk to him."

"Your parents studied biochemistry at Trinity?" Patrick leaned forward, interested now. "That's brilliant. Did they end up working in the field?"

"They did, actually. Pharmaceutical companies."

"See?" Emily elbowed Patrick triumphantly. "I told you your grandad's wrong. Our degree isn't useless."

Patrick rolled his eyes. "My grandad thinks anything that doesn't involve farming or construction is useless. Where do your parents work now? Still in pharma?"

The question hung in the air like a wrong note. Hazel took another sip of water, buying time to find the right words.

"They died when I was two. Car accident."

The couple's expressions shifted instantly, enthusiasm dimming to sympathy.

"Christ, I'm sorry," Patrick said. "I didn't mean to—"

"It's okay. It was a long time ago." Hazel rotated her water glass, watching condensation bead on its surface. "That's actually why I want to talk to Professor Murphy. He knew them back then, and I'm trying to learn more about their time at Trinity."

An awkward silence settled over them. Emily glanced at Patrick, some silent communication passing between them.

"Table for two?" The hostess had reappeared, professional smile intact. "Your table's ready now."

"Actually," Patrick said, "could we make that three?"

The hostess barely blinked. "Of course. Right this way."

"Oh, no," Hazel protested. "I don't want to intrude on your—"

"Don't be daft," Emily said, already standing. "We can tell you all about Murphy over dinner."

They were already moving toward their table. Hazel grabbed her water and followed, touched by their easy kindness. They did quick introductions while walking—Emily Farrell and Patrick Keoghan, both second-year biochemistry students. Hazel offered her own name, grateful for their openness with a stranger.

Their table was tucked into an alcove beneath an ornate ceiling rose, the kind of architectural detail that belonged in a palace.

Crystal glasses caught the light from the chandeliers, and the heavy silverware suggested serious dining intentions.

"We come here sometimes," Patrick said as they settled in. "Used to be a proper bank—Anglo Irish or something. They kept all the fancy bits when they converted it."

"It's gorgeous." Hazel ran her hand along the polished table edge. "Though I'm surprised students can afford it."

"Ah, we've got a system," Emily said, accepting menus from a waiter who appeared with ninja-like stealth. "Skip the mains, just get the seafood chowder. They list it as a starter, but it's practically a meal. Comes with this amazing brown bread, and it's only twelve euros."

"Twelve euros for soup?"

"Trust us," Patrick said. "You'll understand when you taste it."

The waiter hovered discreetly. They all ordered the chowder, and then Patrick raised an eyebrow at Hazel. "Drinks? You can't visit Ireland without trying a proper Guinness."

"Isn't it a school night? Don't you have that lecture tomorrow?"

"We'll be grand," Emily laughed. "It's tradition—pint on the first night of term. Come on, when in Dublin…"

"When in Dublin, get peer-pressured by students half my age?"

"You're what, thirty?" Patrick guessed. "That's not old. That's like… seasoned."

Seasoned? Maybe a month of murder-solving had aged her. The stress had to show somewhere.

"I'm twenty-five."

"See? Basically our age. Three pints of Guinness," he told the waiter before Hazel could protest further.

"I don't really drink beer," she said after the waiter left.

"Guinness isn't beer," Emily said with mock seriousness. "It's a food group. Practically a meal in itself. Full of iron and nutrients and things."

"Things?"

"Very scientific things. I'm studying biochemistry, I should know."

Their chowder arrived faster than expected, brought by a different waiter who balanced the bowls with impressive skill. The smell hit Hazel first—ocean and cream and something herbed that made her stomach growl audibly.

"Told you," Patrick said as her spoon broke through the thick surface to reveal chunks of fish and potato beneath. "Proper food, this."

Hazel took her first spoonful and hummed in satisfaction. Creamy didn't begin to describe it. The seafood was perfectly cooked, the potatoes yielding but not mushy, and the brown bread that came alongside was dense and nutty and perfect for soaking up every drop.

"This is incredible."

"And you doubted us." Emily tore off a piece of bread with satisfaction. "Twenty euros says you'll be dreaming about this chowder tonight."

Their Guinness arrived in three perfect pints, the creamy head sitting distinct from the dark body below. Hazel regarded hers with suspicion.

"You have to wait," Patrick instructed. "Let it settle. See how the bubbles are still moving? When they stop, it's ready. That's how you know you're in a decent place—they take the time to pour it right."

"There's a whole ritual?"

"Welcome to Ireland," Emily said. "We've got rituals for everything. Pouring pints, making tea, avoiding straight answers to direct questions…"

They chatted while their pints settled, the couple painting a picture of themselves with easy strokes. Both from County Wexford but different towns—hadn't met until Trinity. Second-year students living in on-campus accommodation, which Patrick described as "like prison but with worse food" and Emily corrected to "perfectly adequate if you don't mind sharing a kitchen with people who think washing dishes is optional."

"You should visit Wexford while you're here," Emily suggested. "Gorgeous beaches, proper Irish countryside. Not like Dublin at all."

"I'm only here for a few days," Hazel said. "Research trip."

"Research?" Patrick perked up. "What kind?"

"Family history." It wasn't quite a lie. "My grandmother died recently, and I'm trying to piece together some things about my parents."

"Through Professor Murphy?"

"He's one of the few people still around who knew them. My parents' friend in Rome—long story—suggested I talk to him."

"Rome?" Emily's eyes widened. "God, that's romantic. Trailing across Europe piecing together family mysteries. It's like something from a film."

If only she knew about the murders, Hazel thought. Less romantic, more traumatic.

"Right, they're ready," Patrick announced, examining his pint with the seriousness of a sommelier. "Now, you don't sip Guinness like wine. You take a proper mouthful. But not too big—you're not chugging it like some American beer. Find the middle ground."

Hazel lifted her pint, the glass heavier than expected. The first taste was... actually good. Creamy and slightly bitter, with a complexity that regular beer lacked. It didn't assault her taste buds like the IPAs Mike used to favor.

"Not bad," she admitted.

"Not bad?" Patrick clutched his chest dramatically. "She says 'not bad' about Ireland's greatest contribution to world culture."

"I thought that was Yeats," Emily said.

"Yeats never helped anyone through a breakup at two in the morning."

"Fair point."

They returned to their chowder, and Hazel steered the conversation toward what she really needed to know. "So Professor Murphy—what's he like?"

"Brilliant," Emily said immediately. "Properly brilliant. You know how some professors just read from slides? Murphy barely uses them. He'll start explaining something basic like protein folding and end up connecting it to climate change or ancient Roman medicine or his time working in industry."

"He worked in pharmaceutical companies?"

"Years ago," Patrick confirmed. "Always goes on about it. 'When I was young and working in industry, we developed compounds that changed the field...' Makes us feel like proper children."

"He must be getting up there in age," Hazel ventured.

"Seventy-five and sharp as ever," Emily said. "Swear to God, he remembers every student's name after one class. Bit terrifying, actually. Nowhere to hide if you haven't done the reading."

Patrick coughed pointedly.

"He's strict about academics," Emily continued, ignoring him. "Zero tolerance for cheating. Remember what happened with that lad last year? Caught plagiarizing, Murphy reported him and made sure he failed the module. Had to repeat the entire year. But if you're genuinely trying, he's incredibly supportive."

"Sounds intimidating."

"Nah, he's grand," Patrick said. "Tells the best stories. Like this one time, he was working with a research team here in Dublin, and they accidentally created a compound that made all the lab mice hyperactive. Spent weeks trying to figure out what went wrong, turned out they'd mixed up two similar-looking chemicals."

"Patrick's leaving out the best bit," Emily interrupted. "The mice were so wired they basically destroyed their enclosure overnight. Murphy came in the next morning to find they'd shredded everything shreddable and built what looked like little nests in the corners."

"Sounds chaotic," Hazel laughed.

"That's what makes his lectures great," Emily said. "Real stories from real lab work, even the embarrassing mistakes."

They finished their chowder, scraping bowls clean with the last of the brown bread. Hazel found herself genuinely enjoying their company. They reminded her of what she'd missed by not going to college—the casual friendships, the inside jokes about professors, the sense of being part of something bigger than a small-town bakery.

"We've got his lecture tomorrow," Emily said, as if reading her mind. "First one of term, so it'll probably be pretty relaxed. Overview of what we're covering, expectations, that sort of thing."

"You could come," Patrick suggested. "I mean, if you want to see him in action before trying to talk to him."

"I can't just walk into a university lecture."

"Why not?" Emily leaned forward conspiratorially. "It's the first week of term. Security's completely relaxed, tons of new faces everywhere. One more won't matter."

"But I'm not a student."

"So? It's not like they check IDs at the door. Half the first years don't even have their student cards yet." Patrick polished off his Guinness with satisfaction. "We could meet you outside the Biomedical Sciences building. Walk in together like you belong there."

"Which you sort of do," Emily added. "Your parents were students. You're just... continuing the family tradition. Very late."

The idea was tempting. Seeing Professor Murphy in his element before approaching him would be valuable. She could gauge his personality, maybe catch him after class...

"You're thinking too hard," Emily said. "It's a lecture, not a bank heist. Worst case, someone asks you to leave. Which they won't."

"Okay," Hazel decided. "Yes. That would be amazing, actually."

"Brilliant!" Patrick signaled for the check. "Lecture's at nine. We'll meet you outside the building at quarter to?"

"I'll be there."

The check arrived, and Hazel snatched it before either student could react. "My treat. You're helping me out, and I know the student budget struggle."

"You don't have to—" Emily started.

"I insist. Consider it payment for Professor Murphy intelligence."

They didn't argue too hard, confirming Hazel's suspicion about their finances. Outside, the rain had stopped, leaving the streets shiny and smelling of wet concrete. The couple headed back toward Trinity, probably to whatever passed for adequate student housing, while Hazel turned toward her B&B.

What were the chances? She'd come to Dublin with only a name and a hope of finding Professor Murphy, and within hours she'd stumbled into his actual students. Maybe Dublin was offering her something she hadn't had in Paris or Rome—a bit of luck that didn't involve corpses.

Although knowing her recent history, she'd probably find Professor Murphy face-down in a beaker tomorrow.

No. Stop that. Not every city could have a murder waiting. Statistics alone suggested she was due for a nice, peaceful information-gathering trip. Meet the professor, learn about her parents, move on with new information and no trauma.

She could do this. Tomorrow she'd sit in on a real university lecture for the first time in her life, finally experiencing a taste of the education she'd missed. Then she'd introduce herself to Professor Murphy and hopefully get answers about her parents' research, their time at Trinity, maybe even insights into their deaths.

Simple. Straightforward. Corpse-free.

Famous last thoughts, part two.

8

Hazel woke to the sound of rain pattering against her window. Of course. She checked the weather app: cloudy with a chance of rain all day. At least Irish weather was consistent in its inconsistency.

She showered, grateful for water pressure that didn't require interpretive dance to rinse shampoo. The Rome hotel's shower had been like standing under someone halfheartedly spitting at you. This was proper water pressure, the kind that could wake you up without coffee.

She dressed in layers—long-sleeved shirt, cardigan, light jacket. If Dublin weather wanted to play games, she'd be ready for all of them.

The B&B's dining room was small but welcoming, set with mismatched china that somehow worked together. Mrs. O'Neill bustled out from the kitchen, looking impossibly chipper for seven-thirty in the morning.

"You're up early! First one down, actually. The others are still dead to the world." She set a pot of tea on Hazel's table without asking if she wanted any. Apparently tea wasn't optional in Irish B&Bs. "Full Irish breakfast?"

"Sure." When in Dublin, clog your arteries like the locals.

"Grand. Won't be five minutes."

She disappeared back into the kitchen, leaving Hazel with the tea and her thoughts. The dining room windows looked out onto the street where rain continued its steady patter, turning the morning commuters into a parade of umbrellas.

True to her word, Mrs. O'Neill returned quickly with a plate that could have fed three people. Eggs, bacon, sausages, grilled tomato, mushrooms, some kind of white pudding, the infamous black pudding, and toast cut into triangles like fancy sandwiches.

"Busy day planned?" Mrs. O'Neill hovered, clearly hoping for conversation.

"Meeting an old family acquaintance at Trinity."

"Oh, lovely! Professor, is he? Or she? We get a lot of visiting academics staying here. Close to the college and all."

"Professor, yes." Hazel cut into the black pudding, determined to try it at least once. It tasted... actually nice. Rich and savory with a texture that wasn't as alarming as she'd expected. "Been there quite a while, I think."

"They do tend to stick around, the Trinity lot. Prestigious positions, hard to come by." Mrs. O'Neill adjusted a doily that didn't need adjusting. "Well, I'll leave you to your breakfast. Shout if you need anything!"

Hazel worked her way through the massive meal, managing about two-thirds before admitting defeat. The white pudding was good too, milder than its black cousin. The whole thing was a heart attack on a plate, but a delicious one.

Outside, the rain had paused for its mid-morning break. Hazel headed out, taking the now-familiar route toward Trinity. She'd allowed extra time to walk through campus rather than going directly to the Biomedical Sciences building. Might as well play tourist one more time.

The campus was busier than yesterday afternoon. Students hurried along the paths, backpacks heavy with new textbooks, faces showing the universal expression of "why did I sign up for a nine AM class?" Others stood in groups near building entrances, clutching coffee cups and scrolling through phones.

Hazel found herself envying them. Not the early mornings or the student debt, but the belonging. The casual assumption that they were exactly where they should be, doing exactly what twenty-year-olds did. She'd never had that, going straight from high school to Sunrise Bakery with no transition between.

What would her parents think, seeing her here? Would they be proud that she'd finally made it to their university, even if it was just as a visitor? Or sad that she'd missed out on the full experience they'd had?

She walked through the campus, past old stone buildings and the sports fields, following her phone's GPS directions. The route took her under the elevated DART tracks and out onto city streets. The Biomedical Sciences Institute, when she finally found it, was jarringly modern compared to Trinity's historic architecture. All glass and sharp angles, it looked like it had been beamed in from the future and was slightly embarrassed about it.

Patrick and Emily were already waiting outside, looking remarkably fresh for students who'd been drinking on a school night.

"Morning!" Emily called out. "You found it alright?"

"Hard to miss. It's the one building that looks like it was designed this century."

"Try this millennium," Patrick said. "Opened in 2011."

They headed for the entrance, joining a stream of students filing through the automatic doors. Hazel tensed as they approached what looked like security turnstiles, but Patrick was right—they were all propped open, a bored security guard waving everyone through without a glance.

"First week is chaos," Emily explained as they navigated the corridors. "Half the new students can't find their classrooms, professors are still sorting schedules, nobody knows what's happening. Perfect time to blend in."

The lecture hall was bigger than Hazel had expected, with stadium seating that could probably hold two hundred students. Maybe a third of the seats were already filled, with more trickling in steadily.

"We always sit at the back," Patrick said, leading the way up the steps. "Better view of everyone's panic when Murphy announces surprise quizzes."

"He doesn't actually do surprise quizzes," Emily clarified. "But he likes to threaten them to keep people on their toes."

They settled into seats near the back corner, Hazel sitting beside Patrick and Emily like she belonged there. The lecture hall filled steadily, voices echoing off the high ceiling in a multilingual chorus. She caught Italian accents, French ones, something that might have been German, and plenty of Irish variations.

"International bunch," she commented.

"Trinity's got a good reputation for biochemistry," Emily said. "Plus, EU students pay the same fees as Irish ones, so we get loads from the continent. That girl down there? From Italy, always correcting everyone's pronunciation."

"It's not our fault Latin sounds different with an Irish accent," Patrick muttered.

Hazel glanced at her phone. Two minutes to nine. "Think Professor Murphy might be running late?"

"Murphy? Late?" Emily laughed. "He'll walk through that door at exactly nine o'clock. Always does. And then he'll close it behind him—doesn't let latecomers in at all. Says if you can't respect his time, he won't waste it on you."

"Good thing we got here early then."

"Very good thing. Last term someone showed up thirty seconds late and Murphy wouldn't even acknowledge their knocking. Just kept lecturing like nothing was happening."

Hazel settled back in her seat, pulse quickening slightly. In a few moments, she'd finally see the man who'd known her parents, who might hold the key to understanding their research and their deaths. Cornelius Murphy—brilliant scientist, demanding professor, and possibly her best hope for answers.

Time to see what he was really like.

9

P rofessor Cornelius Murphy's alarm sounded at precisely 7:15 AM, as it had every weekday for the past thirty-seven years. He silenced it on the first beep—never the snooze button, that was for people who lacked discipline—and sat up in his narrow bed. The September morning light was just beginning to filter through his bedroom window, weak and gray but enough to navigate without switching on the lamp.

He padded to the bathroom in his cotton pajamas, feet finding their way without conscious thought. Everything in its place, everything with a purpose. Toothbrush at a forty-five-degree angle in its holder, towel folded in precise thirds on the rail, shower temperature set to exactly thirty-eight degrees Celsius. Some might call it obsessive. He called it efficient.

The shower lasted eight minutes. No more, no less. Enough time to thoroughly clean while not wasting water or, more importantly, time. He dressed in clothes laid out the night before—charcoal trousers, white shirt, navy tie with the Trinity crest. The same combination he wore every Monday during term.

Downstairs, his kitchen gleamed under the fluorescent lights. Stainless steel appliances reflected his movements as he prepared breakfast. Two slices of whole grain toast, butter applied evenly to the edges, marmalade measured out with a teaspoon. Black coffee in his usual mug—a gift from the biochemistry department for his twenty-fifth year of teaching, now chipped but still perfectly functional. He ate standing at the counter, scanning the Irish Times science section.

The house around him bore the marks of a life lived alone by choice. No family photos cluttered the mantelpiece, no partner's belongings disrupted his systems. Just books—hundreds of them, organized first by subject, then alphabetically by author. Scientific journals filled custom-built shelves in what might have been a dining room in a normal home. Here, it served as an auxiliary library.

He'd chosen this path deliberately at thirty-two, when Orla Donnelly had given him her ultimatum: her or the lab. The decision had been surprisingly easy. Love was temporary, unpredictable, messy. Science was eternal, logical, controllable. He'd never regretted it.

Well. Rarely regretted it.

Sometimes, on mornings like this, eating toast alone in a silent kitchen, he wondered what it might have been like. Children asking questions at breakfast, a wife complaining about his tendency to grade papers at the dinner table. Chaos, certainly. But perhaps a warmer sort of chaos than his ordered existence.

He dismissed the thought, rinsing his plate and mug immediately, placing them in their designated spots in the dishwasher. Sentiment was for people who didn't have research papers to review and a lecture to prepare.

His study—the third bedroom converted years ago—contained his work for the day. Quiz papers stacked with military precision, lecture notes reviewed one final time despite knowing them by heart. He'd given this particular lecture seventeen times. But preparation was key. Complacency led to mistakes, and Cornelius Murphy did not make mistakes.

At 8:18 AM, he gathered his materials into his leather briefcase, another artifact from decades past but still perfectly serviceable. Keys from the hook by the door, coat from its designated hanger, umbrella from the stand—September in Dublin demanded preparation for all weather possibilities.

The walk to Blackrock DART station took eleven minutes at his usual pace. He'd timed it repeatedly over the years, factoring in traffic light patterns and pedestrian congestion. The 8:31 train would get him to Dublin Pearse by 8:46, leaving ample time for the five-minute walk to the Biomedical Sciences building.

He checked his watch as he reached the platform. 8:29. Perfect timing, as always. Other commuters huddled against the morning chill, but Murphy stood straight, briefcase at his side, watching the digital display count down to the train's arrival.

8:30 became 8:31.

Then 8:32.

Murphy's jaw tightened. The DART was late. Not catastrophically so, but late nonetheless. This hadn't been factored into his morning schedule. Two minutes might seem trivial to most people, but those people didn't understand the cascading effect of small delays. Two minutes here meant walking faster to the university, arriving slightly breathless, possibly perspiring. Unacceptable.

The train finally arrived at 8:32 and forty-seven seconds. Murphy boarded with the other passengers, irritation simmering beneath his calm exterior. He found his usual seat—third carriage, left side, facing forward—and placed his briefcase on his lap. The office worker beside him was eating a breakfast roll, the smell of sausage and brown sauce overwhelming in the enclosed space. Another disruption to the morning's order.

Fifteen minutes later, the train pulled into Dublin Pearse station. Murphy was first off, striding through the ticket barriers with purpose. The morning air hit him as he emerged onto the street, carrying the scent of rain and exhaust fumes. He increased his pace, long legs eating up the pavement.

Students passed him heading in the same direction, some recognizing him and offering nervous greetings that he acknowledged with curt nods. His watch showed 8:49. Still sufficient time, but the margin for error had shrunk considerably.

His last lateness haunted him still, though it had been over fifty years ago. First year at university, cocky and careless, he'd strolled into Professor Hartwell's organic chemistry lecture five minutes late. The professor had stopped mid-sentence, fixed him with a stare that could have frozen helium, and asked if Mr. Murphy had anything more important to do than attend his lecture.

The humiliation had been complete. Hartwell had made him stand at the front, explaining to the entire class why punctuality mattered in science. "If you're five minutes late adding a reagent, Mr. Murphy, your reaction fails. If you're five minutes late reading a patient's test results, they might die. Science doesn't wait for lazy young men who think the world revolves around their schedule."

He'd never been late again.

The Biomedical Sciences building loomed ahead, all gleaming glass and modern angles. Murphy's pace didn't slow as he pushed through the main doors. The security guard, Declan, looked up from his newspaper.

"Morning, Professor Murphy."

"Declan." A nod, nothing more. No time for the usual pleasantries about weather or sport.

The corridors echoed with his footsteps. Other faculty members greeted him—Dr. Fanning from Pharmacology, Professor Byrne from Molecular Biology—but Murphy offered only brief acknowledgments. Students pressed themselves against walls as he passed, and he caught their whispered conversations in his wake.

"Christ, Murphy looks ready to kill someone."

"Bet someone's getting expelled today."

He wondered, not for the first time, why students seemed to fear him. Yes, he maintained high standards. Yes, he expected excellence. But wasn't that what Trinity College Dublin represented? The best university in Ireland didn't achieve that status by coddling underperformers.

He reached the lecture hall doors and stopped. Two students rushed past him, diving through the doors with seconds to spare.

Murphy pulled out his pocket watch—a graduation gift from his own professor, still keeping perfect time after five decades. He waited, watching the second hand sweep around the face. Thirty seconds to nine... fifteen... ten...

At exactly nine o'clock, he grasped the door handle and entered the lecture hall.

The chatter died instantly. Good. They'd learned from last year's example of Ethan Gallagher, who'd kept talking through Murphy's entrance and found himself asked to leave before the lecture even began.

He walked straight to his desk along the front wall, cataloging faces automatically as he moved. Zoe O'Brien in her usual front-row seat, notebook already open, pen poised. Brilliant girl, possibly the best student he'd taught in years. Several seats away—with that careful distance that spoke of deliberate separation—sat Maeve Delaney, dark hair pulled back severely, jaw set in determination. Another excellent mind, perpetually frustrated by always placing second.

His mental attendance continued. The Italian exchange student who insisted on pronouncing every scientific term with unnecessary flourish. The boy from Carlow who'd barely scraped through first year but showed signs of improvement. The Swedish girl who asked surprisingly insightful questions when she bothered to attend.

And there, in the back corner, Patrick Keoghan with Emily Farrell. He'd have to split them up if their relationship interfered with their studies. Romance was all well and good, but not during his lectures. And next to them—

His step faltered for just a moment.

The resemblance hit him like a physical blow. Dark hair falling in the same waves, the same sharp intelligence in her eyes, the same way of observing rather than just looking, even the slight furrow between her brows that appeared when concentrating. For one impossible moment, he was forty-five again, watching Olivia Robbins debate Thomas Chase about enzyme kinetics in the old biochemistry building.

But Olivia was dead. Had been for over twenty years. He didn't believe in ghosts, had no patience for supernatural nonsense. The dead stayed dead, no matter how much the living might wish otherwise.

So who was this young woman wearing Olivia's face?

10

The lecture hall door opened at precisely nine o'clock. The chatter died instantly as Professor Cornelius Murphy entered, closing the door firmly behind him with the air of someone who'd just locked out any latecomers.

He wasn't what Hazel had expected. Tall and lean, with silver hair that looked more distinguished than elderly, he moved with the energy of someone half his age. His face was lined but alert, sharp blue eyes scanning the room like he was taking attendance mentally.

And then his eyes landed on Hazel, and she saw it—the same expression Charles Lambert had worn when he first saw her in Paris. Like seeing a ghost. Her stomach clenched. Emily had said Murphy remembered every single student's name. What if he decided to kick her out for not belonging here?

But he wouldn't. That moment of recognition, quickly suppressed but unmistakable, told her he'd seen her mother in her face. He wouldn't throw out Olivia's daughter. She was sure of it.

Murphy's pause lasted maybe a second before he continued to his desk, depositing his briefcase with practiced precision. When he turned to face the class, his expression had returned to professional neutrality.

"Good morning, and welcome back to Enzyme Biochemistry." His voice carried easily through the lecture hall without shouting. "I trust you all had productive summers, though given the state of some of your final exams last term, perhaps 'productive' is optimistic."

Nervous laughter rippled through the room.

"Before we discuss this year's curriculum, let's see how much you've retained. A few review questions, shall we?" He moved to the whiteboard, writing with quick, neat strokes. "Can anyone explain the difference between competitive and non-competitive enzyme inhibition?"

A hand shot up in the front row. A blonde girl with pearl earrings and designer clothes, everything about her radiating confidence and privilege.

"Miss O'Brien?"

"Competitive inhibitors bind to the enzyme's active site, directly competing with the substrate. Non-competitive inhibitors bind to an allosteric site, changing the enzyme's conformation and reducing its activity regardless of substrate concentration."

"Correct. And the Michaelis-Menten constant changes how in each case?"

The same hand rose.

"In competitive inhibition, Km appears to increase while Vmax remains unchanged. In non-competitive inhibition, Vmax decreases while Km stays the same."

"Excellent." Murphy turned back to the board. "Now, who can tell me why this matters in drug design?"

Hazel leaned toward Patrick. "Who is that?" she whispered.

"Zoe O'Brien," he murmured back. "Star student. Best in our year, probably best in the whole program. Also quite popular with the lads, if you know what I mean."

Emily's hand found Patrick's, squeezing just hard enough to be noticed. "Patrick."

"What? I'm just answering her question. Not like I'm interested—you're the only one for me, Em."

Hazel smiled despite herself. They were adorable in that nauseating way young couples often were. Like looking at what her parents might have been—young and in love at Trinity, their whole lives stretching ahead.

Murphy continued firing questions at the class. Each time, Zoe's hand rose first, her answers precise and complete. Several seats away, a brunette girl with freckles and worn textbooks piled high on her desk raised her hand a beat behind, frustration building visibly in her shoulders.

"And who's that?" Hazel asked, nodding toward the brunette.

Emily leaned in. "Maeve Delaney. Always second place to Zoe. Sweet girl, works harder than anyone, but…" She shrugged.

"They got into a proper fight once," Patrick added. "Middle of the library, books flying everywhere. Still don't know what set them off."

Fighting over grades. Hazel had worked at Sunrise Bakery since graduating high school, where the biggest conflict was who had to clean the mixer. The idea of caring enough about academic rankings to throw punches seemed like something from another world.

A knock interrupted Murphy's next question. The door opened, and a young man stuck his head in. Athletic build, bleached hair styled in aggressive spikes, the kind of confidence that came from rarely hearing "no."

"Here we go," Patrick muttered. "Cian's done for. Showing up late to Murphy's first lecture?"

"Sorry, Professor," Cian said, not sounding sorry at all. "Can I come in?"

Murphy's expression didn't change, but something in his stillness suggested amusement. "Ah, Mr. Blackburn. How good of you to join us. Tell me, what time does your schedule say this lecture begins?"

"Nine o'clock, Professor."

"And what time is it now?"

"About quarter past?"

"Twenty-five minutes past, to be precise. Nearly a third of the lecture missed. Tell me, Mr. Blackburn, if you arrived twenty-five minutes late to a surgical procedure, would the patient wait for you?"

"I'm not studying medicine—"

"The principle remains. Science operates on precision, Mr. Blackburn. Chemical reactions don't pause for tardy students. Cells don't stop dividing because you hit the snooze button." He paused, letting the words sink in. "You know my policy on latecomers."

Cian shrugged, apparently unbothered. As he turned to leave, he caught sight of Zoe in the front row. She blew him a kiss, subtle but unmistakable.

"Do Zoe and Cian date?" Hazel whispered.

Patrick and Emily exchanged one of those couple looks that conveyed entire conversations.

After a brief pause, Patrick answered, "No, why do you ask?"

"She just blew him a kiss."

Emily's smile looked slightly forced. "You probably just misinterpreted. See that red-haired girl in the middle section, fourth row? That's Aisling Grant, Cian's girlfriend. They've been together since first year."

"Right," Hazel said slowly, though she was certain of what she'd seen. The gesture had been deliberate, practiced. But maybe Dublin students were just more affectionate than she was used to.

Murphy cleared his throat, and the whispered conversations died. "Now that we've dealt with interruptions, let's discuss the reading I assigned for today. I trust everyone completed it?"

Groans echoed through the hall.

"Excellent. Then you'll have no trouble with the quiz I've prepared."

"You've got to be kidding," Patrick hissed. "Emily, you jinxed it yesterday! You said he only threatens quizzes!"

"You should have done the reading," Emily shot back.

"Help me?"

Emily rolled her eyes. "What would you do without me?"

"Fail, probably."

Murphy gestured to the front row. "Pass these back, please. You have until the end of the lecture to complete all questions. This won't count toward your final mark—consider it a diagnostic tool. Though if the results are sufficiently dire, we may need to revisit that decision."

The stack of papers made its way up the rows. Hazel's pulse quickened as she took one. She wasn't a student, had no business being excited about a biochemistry quiz she couldn't possibly pass.

But something about sitting here, surrounded by actual students, made her want to try.

The first question might as well have been written in Mandarin. "Describe the role of ATP synthase in oxidative phosphorylation." She knew ATP was some kind of energy molecule—thank you, high school biology—but synthase? Oxidative what-now?

"You know you can skip it," Patrick whispered, glancing over. "Not like Murphy's expecting a paper from his non-student."

"I want to try."

He shrugged. "Your funeral."

Hazel bent over the paper, writing what she remembered from her frantic pre-Dublin research. Half the answers came from pure guesswork, others from subtle glances at Emily's paper when she shifted positions. By the time Murphy called time, she'd filled in something for every question, even if most of it was probably nonsense.

Students filed toward the front, depositing their quizzes on Murphy's desk. Hazel hung back with Patrick and Emily, joining the end of the queue.

"First lecture and already a quiz," Patrick complained. "Thought we'd have at least a week before the torture started."

"And we've got Professor Byrne's molecular biology lecture next," Emily said with a groan. "She loves surprise quizzes too. The torture never ends. Want to join us, Hazel?"

"Thanks, but I'll try to talk to Professor Murphy," Hazel said. "That's what I came here for, after all. Hopefully he has some free time before his next class."

"Good luck with that." Emily pulled out her phone. "Here, let's exchange numbers. In case you need another rescue mission or just want to grab a pint while you're in Dublin."

They swapped contacts, though Hazel doubted she'd need more help. These two had already done enough, sneaking her into the lecture and making her feel welcome. Whatever came next with Professor Murphy, she'd handle alone.

The last few students deposited their papers and filed out. Hazel approached the desk, quiz in hand, acutely aware this was it—the moment she'd flown to Dublin for.

11

Up close, the resemblance was even more striking. The same delicate bone structure, the way she tucked her hair behind her ear—a gesture he'd seen Olivia make a thousand times during lectures. Even the slight tilt of her head as she approached, nervous but determined.

"Professor Murphy?" Her American accent was unmistakable. "I'm Hazel Chase. I heard you taught my parents years ago—Olivia and Thomas Chase?"

He accepted her quiz paper, scanning it quickly. Earnest attempts at answers, most wrong but showing at least basic scientific literacy. Definitely not her parents' path—Thomas would have aced this quiz in his sleep, and Olivia would have added three pages of additional notes just to show off.

"Miss Chase." He set the paper aside. "Your approach to oxidative phosphorylation is creative, if entirely incorrect."

She flushed. "I'm not really a science person."

"Evidently." He studied her more openly now. "I see both your parents in you. Your mother's eyes—same shade of hazel, actually. Your name suits you perfectly. You have her bone structure and mannerisms too, but your father's nose and that determined set to your jaw when you're concentrating."

"You knew my parents well?"

"Very well indeed." He glanced at the door as new students began filtering in for the next lecture. "I have a break after this class. Perhaps we could continue this conversation somewhere more comfortable? The canteen serves passable coffee and excellent cheesecake, if you're interested."

"That would be perfect."

"Wait outside, then. This lecture runs ninety minutes." He paused. "Unless you'd like to audit this one as well? Though I should warn you, Advanced Protein Biochemistry makes this morning's material look like nursery rhymes."

"I'll wait outside."

He watched her leave, mind already racing ahead to their conversation. What had brought Olivia's daughter to Dublin? And more troubling—why now, after all these years?

The next ninety minutes crawled past. His lecture on protein folding pathways suffered from unusual distraction, though he doubted the students noticed. His standards for "distracted" still exceeded most professors' peak performance.

When he finally dismissed the class, he found Hazel sitting on a bench in the corridor, absorbed in her phone. She looked up as he emerged, and again that echo of Olivia made his breath catch.

"The canteen's this way." He led her through the building's maze of corridors. As they passed a particularly stark stretch of white walls, he gestured vaguely. "Hard to believe your parents had to endure the old biochemistry building. We thought we were lucky to have our own dedicated space, but looking back…"

"What was it like?"

"Freezing in winter, stifling in summer, and the acoustics made every cough sound like thunder. But it had character—high windows, creaking floors, that sort of thing." He held the canteen door open for her. "This building's more functional but rather soulless, don't you think?"

The lunch crowd hadn't arrived yet, leaving them plenty of empty tables. Murphy selected one by the window, away from the main traffic flow. He ordered coffee and cheesecake for both of them—the canteen's cheesecake was legendary among faculty, though he'd never admit to such frivolous opinions.

"So," he said once they were settled, "Hazel Chase. I must admit, seeing you in my lecture hall was quite a shock. You look remarkably like your mother."

"People keep telling me that." She fidgeted with her coffee cup. "Charles Lambert in Paris said the same thing, right before…"

"Before?"

"He was murdered that night. Before he could tell me anything about my parents."

Murphy's coffee cup paused halfway to his lips. "Charles murdered? I read about it—tragic, what happened to him." He set the cup down carefully. "I remember Charles. He was in a different program at Trinity but friends with your parents. Were you there when it happened? Why were you in Paris?"

"It's a long story. Not really relevant now." She waved it away, though Murphy filed the information for later consideration. "I'm trying to learn about my parents. My grandmother died three months ago, and she left me all this money—their money, apparently. But she never told me anything about them, and now I'm finding out they had all these friends across Europe, and there might be more to their deaths than just a car accident, and I don't even know where to start."

The words tumbled out in a rush, twenty-three years of questions finally finding voice. Murphy sipped his coffee, organizing his thoughts. Where to begin indeed?

12

"Your parents," Murphy said, "were two of the most brilliant students I ever taught. Not just academically brilliant, you understand—Trinity's full of clever people. But Thomas and Olivia had something rarer. They genuinely wanted to use science to make the world better."

"Tell me about them. As students, I mean. What were they like?"

Murphy found himself smiling despite the circumstances. "Thomas could look at the most complex theoretical problem and see elegant solutions where others saw only chaos. He'd fill blackboards with equations, completely lost to the world."

"And my mother?"

"Olivia was the practical one. She'd take Thomas's beautiful theories and figure out how to actually implement them in the lab.

'That's all very nice, Tom,' she'd say, 'but how do we actually make it work?' They balanced each other perfectly—like two halves of the same brilliant mind."

Hazel leaned forward, hungry for details. "When did they start dating?"

"Almost immediately. They met during orientation week, and by October they were inseparable. Other students used to joke that they'd been manufactured as a matching set. They'd sit together in every lecture, finish each other's sentences, debate biochemistry like other couples discussed films."

He paused, remembering. "They had their own language, almost. Half-sentences and shared looks that conveyed entire conversations. Rather annoying during lectures, actually—they'd have these silent debates while I was trying to teach."

Hazel smiled, but it carried sadness. "I grew up with none of that. My grandmother barely mentioned them, and when she did, it was just basic facts. They died when I was two, that's all I knew."

"Bridget was always protective," Murphy said carefully. "Even when Thomas was a student. She'd call him every Sunday, make sure he was eating properly, not staying up too late in the lab. Thomas would complain to Olivia about it, but he always took the calls."

"You knew my grandmother?"

"Only through Thomas's stories and the few times she visited. Formidable woman. I remember she attended Thomas's thesis defense, sat in the front row like a security guard. I think she was ready to physically fight anyone who challenged her son too harshly."

"That sounds like Bridget." Hazel's voice went soft. "She raised me after they died. Kept me safe, maybe too safe. I never even left California until last month."

Murphy studied her over his coffee cup. Same features as Olivia, but tempered by something else—a wariness her mother had never possessed. Life had been kinder to Olivia, at least until the end.

"It's a shame you didn't follow their path," he said. "University, I mean. You clearly have intelligence, and with loans available—"

"I know." She cut him off, then looked apologetic. "Sorry. It's just... I've been thinking the same thing lately. I never pushed for it, and Bridget never suggested it. Now I'm twenty-five and all I've known since graduating high school is working at the bakery. Everyone else my age has degrees, careers, and I'm just..."

"It's never too late to start."

"Maybe." She didn't sound convinced. "Can I ask you something specific? About my parents' work?"

"Of course."

"My grandmother left me this fortune when she died—apparently my parents transferred money to her account right before their car accident. Vittoria Rossi, another friend of theirs who I met in Rome, said she thought it came from their pharmaceutical research. Do you know where the money actually came from?"

Murphy nodded. "Your parents were recruited straight from their PhD programs by a company in California—Golden State Pharmaceuticals. They developed several important compounds, particularly in neurodegenerative disease treatment. Their work led to three major patents. Against my advice, they sold the patent rights outright to the company for a large lump sum instead of taking percentage royalties on future sales."

"Why did you advise against it?"

"Royalties would have paid them far more over time. Those medications are still widely prescribed today—they'd be receiving checks for life. But they wanted the immediate capital, said they had plans." He shrugged. "I assume the money sat in your grandmother's account all these years, accumulating interest."

"That's what her lawyer said. Twenty-three years of compound interest turned their settlement into quite a fortune." Hazel paused. "So they were already financially secure. Why leave California for Amsterdam?"

"That's what surprised everyone. They had excellent positions, groundbreaking research, financial independence. But they were headhunted by Haldrek Pharmaceuticals—a German pharmaceutical company with facilities across Europe. They offered them positions at their Amsterdam research facility. Very prestigious opportunity, cutting-edge research, significant resources. They were thrilled, at first."

"At first?"

"The communication changed after they moved. We'd been in regular contact while they were in California—emails, phone calls, I consulted regularly on their research projects. But Amsterdam..." He shrugged. "Their messages became infrequent, then stopped altogether."

"Why?"

"I assumed they were simply busy. New country, demanding work, possibly confidentiality agreements. It wasn't unusual in pharmaceutical research. But looking back..."

"You think something was wrong?"

"I don't know. That's the truthful answer, Miss Chase. I don't know what happened in Amsterdam, why they stopped communicating, or why they transferred money to your grandmother just before the accident."

Hazel pushed cheesecake around her plate, thinking. "Do you think the accident was really an accident?"

The question he'd asked himself for twenty-three years. "I wanted to believe it was. Easier that way. But certain events suggested otherwise."

"What events?"

"About a month after their deaths, two men visited my office. They claimed to be from Haldrek's legal department, tying up loose ends. But their questions were... odd. They wanted to know if your parents had sent me any research materials, any documents or data from their current projects. When I said no, they became quite insistent. Intimidating, even."

Hazel straightened. "The same thing happened to Vittoria Rossi in Rome. Men asking questions, making threats."

"It happened to her too?"

"I'm guessing they visited anyone who'd been close to my parents." She met his eyes. "Professor, what do you think they were working on?"

"I genuinely don't know. Haldrek was secretive about their research programs, and your parents honored that secrecy. Their last real communication was a Christmas card from Amsterdam, saying they were well and the work was 'challenging but important.' Three months later, they were dead."

"So you think Haldrek might have been involved? Maybe they discovered something the company wanted to suppress?"

Murphy spread his hands. "It's possible. But Miss Chase—Hazel—it's been over twenty years. Whatever truth exists is likely buried deep. And if powerful people wanted your parents silenced then, they certainly won't welcome questions now."

"I can't just let it go." Her jaw set in a way that was purely Thomas—that stubborn determination that had seen him through countless failed experiments. "They were my parents. I never knew them, and now I find out their deaths might not have been accidental? I have to try."

"What do you intend to do?"

"Go to Amsterdam. Visit Haldrek Pharmaceuticals. See what I can find out."

Murphy felt a chill that had nothing to do with the canteen's air conditioning. "That could be dangerous."

"Maybe. But I've made it this far." She managed a weak smile. "Two cities, two murders solved. I'm getting good at this."

"Two murders?"

"Long story. The point is, I need to know the truth. Can you tell me anything else? Anything that might help?"

He considered what he knew, what might be useful versus what might put her in danger. But looking at her face—Olivia's stubbornness combined with Thomas's determination—he knew she'd go regardless.

"Haldrek Pharmaceuticals is still operating," he said finally. "They've grown considerably since your parents' time. The CEO then was Friedrich Kaltmann. He retired about five years ago due to health issues, and his son runs the company now. They specialize in neurological treatments, some cancer research. Very profitable, very private."

"Do you have any contacts there?"

"None. Your parents were my only connection to that company. After their deaths and those visitors, I made a point of avoiding Haldrek entirely." He paused. "Hazel, I understand the need for answers. But sometimes the past should stay buried. Your parents wouldn't want you putting yourself at risk."

"How do you know what they'd want?" The sharpness in her voice surprised them both. "Sorry. I just... I don't even know who they were, not really. Maybe they'd want me to find the truth. Maybe they'd be proud that I'm trying."

Murphy had no answer for that. He'd thought he knew Thomas and Olivia, but they'd kept secrets even from him. Who was he to say what they'd want for their daughter?

A commotion in the corridor interrupted his thoughts. Students were gathering, voices raised in excitement or alarm. Through the glass doors, he could see people running.

"What's happening?" Hazel stood, craning to see.

A student burst through the canteen doors, face flushed with exertion or shock. "Professor Murphy! Something's happened to Zoe O'Brien!"

Murphy was already moving. "What kind of something?"

"I don't know, she collapsed in the bathroom."

But Murphy was already through the doors, Hazel close behind. His mind raced through possibilities—seizure, allergic reaction, acute illness. Zoe had seemed fine during the lecture, but stress could trigger hidden conditions.

They followed the crowd down the corridor toward the ground floor bathrooms. Students clustered around the entrance, some crying, others filming with their phones despite security trying to stop them. Murphy pushed through with the authority of decades of teaching.

"Stand back, all of you. Let me through."

Inside the bathroom, he found chaos. Zoe O'Brien lay crumpled on the tile floor, her perfect blonde hair spread like a halo around her head, blood pooling beneath. But it was the angle of her neck, the absolute stillness of her chest, that told him everything.

The girl who'd answered every question with such confidence just hours ago would never speak again.

13

Not again.

The thought knocked the air from Hazel's lungs. She stared at Zoe O'Brien's still form, blonde hair fanned across the tiles like some macabre art installation. This couldn't be real. She had to be seeing things, some kind of stress-induced hallucination brought on by too much travel and not enough sleep.

But no. The body was real. The shocked faces around her were real. The absolute stillness where life should have been—that was devastatingly real.

Third city. Third body.

Her hands started shaking. In Paris, she'd found Charles Lambert with a dagger in his chest. In Rome, she'd seen Davide Romano's broken body just after he fell from the Colosseum's second level. And now Dublin had offered up Zoe O'Brien, sprawled on a bathroom floor with blood pooling beneath her head.

Detective Arnaud's words from Paris echoed in her memory: *"Do you make a habit of discovering bodies, Mademoiselle Chase?"* She'd laughed it off then, nervous laughter masking the absurdity of the question. Who had a habit of discovering bodies? Serial killers and homicide detectives, that's who. Not small-town bakers from California who'd never left their home state before last month.

But here she was, standing near her third corpse in as many cities. Maybe Arnaud had been onto something. Maybe she was one of those people who regularly stumbled over dead bodies, like some kind of walking murder magnet.

At least she hadn't been the one to find Zoe. Hazel had been safely in the canteen with Professor Murphy, discussing her parents over cheesecake. Same building, yes, but she hadn't discovered the body this time.

Small mercies.

Still, being in the vicinity felt like a pattern. Three European cities, three murders, three times she'd been close enough to hear the screams or see the aftermath. What were the odds? Astronomical, probably. Professor Murphy could calculate them—he seemed like the type who'd find comfort in statistical improbabilities.

Like Murphy, she didn't believe in the supernatural. Ghosts, curses, fate—all nonsense designed to make random events seem meaningful. But three bodies in three cities was starting to test even her skepticism. Was there something wrong with her? Some invisible mark that attracted violence like moths to flame?

She could already hear Janet's voice: "Girl, you need to get your aura cleansed. Find yourself a good psychic, maybe burn some sage. There's definitely something following you around Europe."

Except that wasn't how it worked. In Paris, Louis would have murdered Charles regardless of her presence. His fifteen-year revenge plan had been set in motion long before she'd enrolled in that pastry course. The Rome conspirators had planned Davide's death for months, synchronizing their movements and alibis with military precision. Her attendance on that Colosseum tour had been pure coincidence.

If anything, she'd been in the right place at the right time. Without her, those murders might never have been solved. Louis could have disappeared into the Parisian night. The Rome conspirators could have maintained their perfect alibi. Her presence had brought justice, not death.

So what about Dublin? What about Zoe O'Brien, who'd answered every question perfectly just hours ago? Who would want her dead? The blood pooling beneath her head suggested a fall with significant impact. No visible wounds, no signs of struggle that Hazel could see from her position near the doorway.

An accident? Possible. People slipped in bathrooms all the time. Wet floors, sudden dizziness, a moment's inattention—any of those could send someone tumbling. But something felt off. Maybe it was too convenient, too neat. Maybe this wasn't as simple as it appeared.

Stop it. She was already sliding into investigation mode, cataloging details and possibilities like she had any business playing detective. She didn't need to solve anything this time. Professor Murphy had given her exactly what she'd come for—information about her parents, leads to follow, a new destination in Amsterdam. She should be on her way to the airport, not standing in a university bathroom staring at another corpse.

Her parents had developed important compounds. Sold the patents for a fortune instead of taking royalties—a decision Murphy still questioned decades later. They'd left comfortable positions in California for mysterious work in Amsterdam. And then, right before their deaths, they'd transferred everything to Bridget.

So many questions still to unravel. Why leave California? What was so special about the Amsterdam opportunity? Why the sudden money transfer? And most importantly—was their car accident really an accident, or had those intimidating visitors been right to come asking questions?

Amsterdam held answers. She'd already decided to go, had started mentally packing even as Murphy spoke. It had seemed so easy, finally getting information without anyone dying. Charles had been murdered before he could tell her about her parents. But Murphy had survived their entire conversation, even treated her to cheesecake. Progress.

Until now.

Professor Murphy knelt beside Zoe's body, his academic composure cracking like ice under spring sun. His hands hovered near her neck, not quite touching, as if he could somehow bring her back to life through sheer proximity. The fluorescent lights caught the moisture gathering in his eyes.

Star student. Best in the program. The way she'd answered those questions—eager, brilliant, absolutely certain of her place in the world. Had Murphy seen Olivia in her too? Another brilliant young woman with her whole future mapped out, unaware how quickly futures could be erased?

Hazel moved without thinking, placing her hand on Murphy's shoulder. The fabric of his jacket was rough beneath her palm, his shoulder rigid with suppressed emotion.

"There's nothing you can do anymore," she said softly.

She helped him to his feet, feeling his unsteadiness as he rose from the hard floor. His nod was barely perceptible, acknowledgment without words. When he blinked, a single tear escaped, quickly wiped away with the back of his hand.

"Declan," he called, voice steady despite everything. "You've called the Gardaí?"

The security guard nodded vigorously. "First thing, Professor. They'll be here any moment now."

Gardaí. Right. Irish police. She'd seen their cars around the city, wondered about the name, Googled it after getting back to the B&B yesterday. The full name was Garda Síochána, which translated from Irish as "guardians of the peace."

Guards. Who would definitely have questions about the American non-student lurking in the biomedical building when a student died. Questions she didn't have good answers for beyond "I snuck into a lecture and happened to be nearby when someone died, but I swear this happens to me all the time, ask Detective Arnaud in Paris."

Yeah, that would go over well.

Suddenly Amsterdam seemed very far away and very appealing. She could slip out now, before the Gardaí arrived. Take a taxi to the airport, catch the next flight to the Netherlands, leave Dublin's problems to Dublin's police. She'd done her part in Paris and Rome. Wasn't it someone else's turn to solve a murder?

But Murphy's tear had done something to her resolve. He'd been kind, generous with his memories, patient with her questions. The least she could do was stay until he was okay. Answer whatever questions the Gardaí had, provide moral support, make sure he had someone to talk to who understood the weight of unexpected death.

Even if it meant explaining, once again, why bodies seemed to follow her across Europe like very persistent tourists.

14

Staying had its benefits. While they waited for the Gardaí, information rippled through the growing crowd like gossip at a small-town diner. Hazel positioned herself near the edge of the group, close enough to hear but far enough to avoid seeming ghoulish.

Aisling Grant had found the body. The same Aisling whom Emily had pointed out during the lecture, Cian Blackburn's girlfriend. She'd simply needed the bathroom during the hour-long break after morning lectures ended, pushed open the door, and found Zoe sprawled across the tiles. Her scream had brought people running from all directions.

"Lost consciousness and fell," one student theorized, his voice carrying the authority of someone who'd watched too many medical dramas. "Happens all the time. Low blood sugar, dehydration, stress from the new term starting."

"Could've been pushed," another countered. "That angle doesn't look natural."

"Who'd want to push Zoe? Everyone loved her."

A snort from somewhere in the crowd. "Yeah, right. Everyone loved the girl who made them all look stupid in every class."

Declan, trying to maintain order, shared the detail that made Hazel's stomach clench: "Won't be easy figuring out who was in there with her. This whole section's got a camera blind spot. Budget cuts, they said. We'll fix it next year, they said."

Of course it did. Just like there being no cameras at all inside the pastry school in Paris. Just like the Colosseum cameras being down for maintenance when Davide fell. Because why would Dublin break the pattern now?

The Gardaí arrived in a rush of uniforms and authority, sectioning off the bathroom with yellow tape that looked the same in every country. They moved with practiced efficiency—secure the scene, interview witnesses, establish a timeline. Hazel found herself in a queue of students waiting to give statements, wondering if she should mention her unusual expertise in finding bodies.

Probably not.

"You were in the canteen when this happened?"

The female Garda was younger than Hazel, maybe twenty-three, with red hair pulled back in a regulation bun and the kind of freckles that suggested she burned rather than tanned. Her notebook was already half-full of statements.

"Yes, with Professor Murphy. We heard the commotion, saw students running, and came to see what was happening."

"Can Professor Murphy confirm this?"

"Of course."

"And you're a student here?"

The question she'd been dreading. "No. I'm... visiting. From America. California, specifically. My parents studied here years ago, and Professor Murphy was their teacher. I wanted to meet him, learn about their time at Trinity."

The Garda's pen paused. "So you're not a student, but you were in the building because...?"

"Professor Murphy invited me to coffee after his lecture. Which I attended. With his knowledge." True enough, even if the order of events was slightly rearranged.

"I see." She didn't look like she saw at all. "And you attended his lecture because you're interested in biochemistry?"

"My parents were biochemists. I wanted to see what their classes might have been like." Also true, if incomplete.

"Right." The pen moved steadily across the paper. "And during the lecture, did you notice anything unusual about the victim? Any signs of illness, distress, conflict with other students?"

"She seemed fine. Better than fine, actually. She answered every question Professor Murphy asked, really knew her stuff. I remember thinking she must be the star student because she was so confident, so prepared."

"Any interactions with other students that stood out?"

Hazel hesitated. The air kiss to Cian was probably nothing, a misunderstanding on her part. But in murder investigations—if this was murder—everything mattered.

"There was this moment when a student came in late. Cian Blackburn. Professor Murphy wouldn't let him in, you know, because of his lateness policy. As Cian was leaving, Zoe—the victim—she blew him a kiss. It seemed odd because I'd heard Cian has a girlfriend. Actually, the girl who found the body. Aisling Grant."

The Garda's pen moved faster. "You're very observant for a tourist attending a random lecture."

Heat crept up Hazel's neck. "I'm naturally nosy. Character flaw."

"Hmm." The Garda made another note. "Any reason you stayed after discovering what happened? Most tourists would want to get as far away as possible from something like this."

Good question. *Because I've developed an unfortunate habit of solving murders across Europe* seemed like the wrong answer.

"Professor Murphy was upset. His student had just died. It felt wrong to leave him alone."

The Garda studied her for a moment longer, then snapped her notebook shut. "We may need to contact you again. Are you staying in Dublin long?"

"A few days. I'm at The Liffey Rose B&B."

"Enjoy the rest of your visit. Try to avoid any more crime scenes."

If only it were that easy.

Hazel found Murphy standing by a window, staring out at the September gray like it might offer answers. His reflection in the glass looked older somehow, the lines around his eyes deeper.

"How are you holding up?" she asked.

He turned, seeming surprised she was still there. "I should be asking you that. This can't be the Dublin visit you were expecting."

"I'm starting to expect the unexpected." She joined him at the window. Students milled about outside, some huddled in small groups, others taking selfies with the Gardaí cars in the background. Death as social media content. "I'm sorry about Zoe. She was clearly an exceptional student."

"She was. Best student I've had in years." His voice carried the weight of absolute certainty. "She reminded me of your mother, actually. Same hunger for knowledge, same ability to see connections others missed. I'd hoped…"

He trailed off, but Hazel could fill in the blanks. Hoped to see her graduate, pursue research, maybe change the world the way Thomas and Olivia might have.

"Thank you for staying," he said. "Most people would have fled at the first sign of Gardaí."

"Yeah, well, I've had practice."

He gave her a sharp look. "You mentioned that earlier. Solving murders in Paris and Rome. I assumed you were joking."

"I wish." She rubbed her forehead, feeling a headache building. "It's a long story. Stories, plural. The short version is that I've stumbled into two murder investigations since leaving California, and somehow ended up solving them. Mostly through luck and stubbornness."

"Tell me."

The intensity in his voice surprised her. "Now? Here?"

"If you don't mind. I find myself needing a distraction from... this." He gestured toward the bathroom, still sealed with yellow tape.

So Hazel told him. Charles Lambert's murder and Louis's fifteen-year revenge plan. The Colosseum conspiracy and Margrit's last-minute crisis of conscience. She kept it brief, clinical almost, focusing on facts rather than feelings. How she'd pieced together clues, followed connections, confronted killers who'd started as victims themselves.

When she finished, Murphy was staring at her with an expression she couldn't read.

"Why do you ask?" she said. "Do you think Zoe was murdered?"

"I think—" He stopped as fresh commotion erupted near the building entrance. A woman's voice, high and desperate, cut through the general noise.

"WHERE IS MY DAUGHTER?"

Zoe's mother. Had to be. The same blonde hair, the same elegant features, shaped by years of professional life and now cracking under grief. She moved through the crowd like a force of nature, students parting before her momentum.

Hazel stepped back, giving Murphy space to handle what came next. But she couldn't help wondering if he'd been about to say what she was already thinking.

That Zoe O'Brien's death was no accident.

That Dublin had one more murder for her to solve.

15

Riona O'Brien hadn't gotten where she was by answering every phone call. Director of Clinical Research at Liffey Therapeutics didn't happen by accident—it took focus, dedication, and the ability to ignore distractions.

Her phone vibrated against her desk for the third time in ten minutes. Same number, no caller ID she recognized. Probably spam. Or worse, someone trying to sell her laboratory equipment she didn't need at prices she wouldn't pay.

She adjusted her laptop screen, pulling up the next slide in her presentation. The board meeting was in two hours, and every detail had to be perfect. The new drug trial results were promising—breakthrough promising—but the board would pick apart any weakness in her data.

The phone started again. Fourth call.

For a moment, she considered answering just to tell them to stop calling. But Professor Murphy's voice echoed across the decades: *"When you're working, work. The world won't end if you don't answer every summons immediately."*

He'd been right then, was probably still right now. The only person she'd answer for during work hours was Zoe, and Zoe knew better than to call unless it was an emergency. They had dinner together every evening where they properly caught up on each other's days. Living together meant constant contact, making work interruptions unnecessary.

She smiled despite her concentration. Zoe following in her footsteps, choosing biochemistry, ending up in Murphy's classroom just like she had all those years ago. Time really was circular. Maybe Zoe would even—

A knock interrupted her thoughts. Her assistant, Liam, peered around the door with an expression that made her stomach drop.

"Riona? The Gardaí called. There's been an incident at Trinity. With Zoe."

The words didn't make sense. "What kind of incident?"

"They said..." Liam swallowed, looking everywhere but at her. "Some kind of accident at the college. She's... they said she's dead."

The laptop screen blurred. Her hands found the desk edge, gripping hard enough to hurt.

"That's not possible." Her voice came out steady, professional. The same tone she used to reject flawed hypotheses. "They must have made a mistake. Mixed up students."

"Riona—"

"It's not Zoe." She stood, muscle memory locating her car keys in her purse. "I'll go down there and sort this out. When they realize their error, someone's getting fired."

"Should I reschedule the board meeting?"

"Only if I'm not back in time." She was already moving, heels clicking against the tile with metronomic precision. "Which I will be. Because this is a mistake."

She tried calling Zoe while walking to her car. Straight to voicemail. She tried twice more while starting the engine. Same result.

The drive from Liffey Therapeutics to Trinity usually took twenty-five minutes. She made it in fifteen, running two red lights and discovering her Audi could take corners at speeds the manufacturer probably hadn't intended. Other drivers honked, gestured, swerved to avoid her racing form. She didn't care.

Zoe was fine. Had to be fine. They'd had dinner just yesterday, talked about her courses, her plans for the term. She'd been excited about Murphy's advanced class, already planning her thesis topic. Girls who planned their thesis topics in second year didn't just die on random Monday afternoons.

But the Gardaí cars clustered outside the Biomedical Sciences building suggested otherwise. Real cars meant a real incident. Her hands shook as she parked—badly, diagonally across two spaces—and ran for the entrance.

"I'm Dr. Riona O'Brien," she told the guard at the door. "My daughter—they called about my daughter. Where is she?"

The guard's expression told her everything she didn't want to know. "Ma'am, if you'll come with me. The detectives need—"

"Where is Zoe?"

"Ma'am—"

"WHERE IS MY DAUGHTER?"

The shout echoed off the modern glass and steel, drawing stares from the gathered crowd.

"This way," the guard said gently. "They need you to... to make an identification."

Identification. Such a clinical word. She'd used it in compound analysis, patient screening, but never for this. Now it meant looking at a body and confirming it was the daughter she'd raised alone after Brendan left. The baby who'd grabbed her finger in the delivery room. The child who'd demanded bedtime stories about molecules. The teenager who'd announced she wanted to be just like her mother.

Each step down the corridor felt like walking through quicksand. Her rational mind kept insisting this was all wrong. Zoe had been perfect at dinner. Perfect this morning when she'd left for university, grabbing an apple and promising to tell her about Murphy's lecture later.

Perfect children didn't end up needing identification.

The bathroom door stood open, yellow tape creating a barrier that seemed both flimsy and absolute. Inside, she could see figures in uniform, equipment she recognized from crime shows Zoe liked to mock for their scientific inaccuracies.

And there, on the floor—

"No." The word came out as a whisper, then louder. "No, no, no—"

But the blonde hair was exactly the right shade. The pearl earrings were the ones Riona had given her for her eighteenth birthday. The navy sweater was the one they'd bought together last month, Zoe joking about how it almost matched Trinity's blue and now she looked properly collegiate.

Her legs gave out. Someone caught her—the guard, maybe, or one of the detectives. They were saying things about being sorry for her loss, about needing confirmation that this was Zoe O'Brien, about procedures and investigations.

"It's her." The words felt like swallowing glass. "That's my daughter."

16

They led Riona to a bench in the corridor, someone pushing a paper cup of water into her hands. She stared at it, wondering why people always offered water in crises. As if hydration could fix a broken world.

"Riona."

She looked up to find Professor Murphy standing over her. Older now than when she'd been his student—silver-haired instead of the dark brown from her university days, but still carrying himself with that particular mixture of authority and awkwardness that marked career academics.

"She was brilliant in lecture this morning," he said, sitting beside her with careful movements. "Answered every question, eager as always. I never imagined…"

"She was alive four hours ago." Riona heard her own voice as if from a distance. "How can she be dead now? That's not how time works. That's not how anything works."

"I know. I'm so very sorry."

She lifted her head, really looking at him for the first time. His eyes were red-rimmed, grief etching new lines in his familiar face. But it was the woman standing behind him who made her breath catch.

The same dark hair. The same shade of hazel eyes. The same way of holding herself, alert and watchful, that Riona remembered from decades ago.

Stress was making her hallucinate. That was the only explanation.

"Olivia?"

The woman stepped forward, shaking her head. "I'm Hazel. Hazel Chase. Olivia was my mother. I'm so sorry about your daughter."

The world tilted, righted itself, tilted again. "You're Thomas and Olivia's daughter?"

"Yes. I came to Dublin to talk to Professor Murphy about my parents." She hesitated, then added, "Did you know them?"

Murphy cleared his throat. "Riona was in their year at Trinity. Same program, many of the same classes. I should have mentioned—but with everything happening—"

"Your parents were good people." The words came automatically, the kind of thing you said when someone mentioned dead relatives. But they were also true. Thomas and Olivia had been the couple everyone envied, brilliant and in love and somehow making it look easy.

"Thank you." Hazel paused, searching for appropriate words. "Your daughter—from what I saw in lecture—she stood out even to someone like me who knows nothing about biochemistry."

Fresh tears burned Riona's eyes. This stranger had seen Zoe alive more recently than her own mother. Had watched her answer questions, demonstrate her knowledge, be her spectacular self one last time.

Murphy shifted beside her, that particular movement that meant he was about to say something significant. She'd learned to recognize it during years of lectures.

"Riona, this won't bring Zoe back. Nothing can. But I may have an idea about how to find out what really happened to her."

The tears stopped. "The guards said it was an accident."

"Perhaps. But certain things bother me. The way she fell—if someone simply fainted, they'd crumple. The angle suggests she fell backward with force. A slip might cause that, but on dry tiles? And bathrooms aren't typically fatal unless there's significant impact."

"If someone hurt my daughter—" Rage, clean and sharp, cut through the grief. "If this wasn't an accident, if someone did this to her, I'll—"

"Let's not get ahead of ourselves." Murphy's voice carried the same tone he'd used to calm overeager students. "But I believe Miss Chase here might be able to help us find the truth."

"Me?" The woman—Hazel, Olivia's daughter—looked alarmed. "I'm not—I don't—"

"You solved two murders," Murphy said. "One in Paris, one in Rome."

"Could we maybe not advertise that?" Hazel glanced around nervously. "And they were mostly luck. Being in the right place, asking the right questions. I'm not a detective."

"No. You're something better." Murphy leaned forward, professor in full lecture mode. "My role here is clear—I teach, I guide academic progress, I maintain professional boundaries. I don't delve into my students' personal lives. I don't hear the gossip or see the social dynamics. Zoe was my best student, but that also made her a target. Academic jealousy, personal conflicts, romantic entanglements—none of that reaches me in my office."

"So you're saying students might tell me things they wouldn't tell you?"

"You already got Patrick and Emily to help you. Convinced them to sneak you into my lecture. That's more social connection than I've managed in decades of teaching."

"That was pure chance. We just met at a restaurant and—"

"Chance or not, you're here." Riona found herself leaning forward, hope cutting through grief like sunlight through storm clouds. "Zoe never shared her problems with me. Only her successes, her achievements. If someone was threatening her, if she was frightened..."

The woman was already shaking her head, but Riona pressed on.

"I know she was hiding something. Call it mother's intuition or paranoia, but she'd been different lately. Distracted. If you could find out what happened, find out why—"

"I'll help."

The simple words stopped Riona's breath. This stranger, this echo of the past, was offering what she desperately needed: someone willing to dig deeper, to search for the truth about Zoe's last moments.

"Thank you," she whispered.

Hazel Chase looked uncomfortable, uncertain, somehow young despite being a few years older than Zoe had been. But there was something else in her eyes—determination, maybe, or resignation.

"I've already done this twice," she said quietly. "What's once more?"

Riona gripped the paper cup hard enough to dent it, water sloshing dangerously close to the rim. Four hours ago, Zoe had been alive. In four hours more, maybe they'd know why she wasn't.

Time didn't work the way it should anymore.

But perhaps, with help from the past, they could make sense of the present.

17

The rain started falling the moment Hazel stepped outside the Biomedical Sciences building, as if Dublin's weather had been waiting for the appropriately tragic moment to unleash itself. She fumbled with her umbrella, the mechanism sticking before finally springing open with enough force to nearly take out a passing student.

Perfect. Just perfect.

A crowd of onlookers still clustered near the entrance, phones out, necks craning for a glimpse of something—anything—that might make their social media feeds more interesting. Three Garda cars sat at odd angles, their blue lights painting wet pavement in rhythmic pulses. One officer stood guard at the door, politely but firmly turning away anyone without legitimate business inside.

Ten minutes ago, she'd been sitting with Professor Murphy and Riona O'Brien, agreeing to help investigate a death that shouldn't have been her problem. Riona had lasted maybe thirty seconds after that before the crying started again—deep, body-shaking sobs that made Hazel's chest tight with secondhand grief. The woman's brief moment of clarity, that scientist's need to understand the how rather than accept the what, had crumbled like wet tissue paper.

Hazel couldn't blame her. If anything, she was impressed Riona had managed to think at all after learning about Zoe. Maybe it helped to see a familiar face—or at least an echo of one. Hazel wearing her mother's features like a Halloween mask, showing up right when Riona's world imploded.

Scientists' minds probably did work differently. Even drowning in tragedy, they reached for logic like a life preserver. Murphy dissecting the angle of Zoe's fall while his eyes stayed red-rimmed with loss. Riona pushing through tears to mention her daughter's recent behavior changes. Their brains choosing analysis over acceptance, at least for a few precious moments.

Or maybe that was just being human—focusing on the circumstances because the tragedy itself was too big to swallow whole.

Murphy had pressed both his and Riona's numbers into her phone before she left, making her promise to call with any discoveries. He'd stayed behind to manage the situation, to be the steady academic presence while chaos swirled around him. Hazel had escaped while she could, before anyone thought to ask harder questions about the American tourist who kept showing up near dead bodies.

Her feet found their own way back toward Trinity campus, the route already familiar even after just one day in Dublin. The umbrella drummed a steady rhythm above her head—pat-pat-pat-pat—oddly soothing in its monotony. She needed the white noise, needed something to focus on besides the image of Zoe O'Brien's perfect stillness on those bathroom tiles.

Dublin had given her exactly what she'd come for. Professor Murphy had filled in crucial gaps about her parents—their work, their patents, their move to Amsterdam. She should be booking a flight right now, chasing down the next lead at Haldrek Pharmaceuticals. Instead, all she could think about was a brilliant girl who'd never answer another question, never blow another secret kiss, never frustrate her rivals by being effortlessly perfect.

Hazel stopped at a crosswalk, waiting for the pedestrian signal while rain ran off her umbrella in thin streams. Why had she agreed to investigate? The question nagged at her like a toothache.

Curiosity, partly. The same itch that had driven her to uncover the truth in Paris and Rome. But this felt different. She'd been planning to walk away from Zoe's death, to let Dublin's police handle Dublin's problems. She barely knew the girl—had watched her shine in the morning lecture, answering every question with perfect confidence. That air kiss to Cian had been the only glimpse of personality beneath the academic perfection.

But then Riona had arrived, and everything shifted.

Riona who'd studied with Hazel's parents. Riona whose daughter might have been Hazel's friend in some alternate timeline where car accidents didn't orphan toddlers. If Thomas and Olivia had lived, if they'd stayed in touch with their Trinity classmates, their daughters might have grown up writing emails across the Atlantic. Comparing notes about their brilliant parents, complaining about expectations, maybe even visiting during summer breaks.

That possibility—that ghost of a friendship that never was—had hooked into Hazel's chest and pulled.

The desperation in their voices had sealed her decision. Two brilliant scientists, probably used to solving any problem through logic and experimentation, suddenly faced with one that wouldn't yield to their methods. They needed someone who could slip between the cracks of university life, who could get students to open up about things they'd never tell a professor or a grieving mother.

They needed her. The baker without a degree, the accidental detective who'd stumbled into solving murders through sheer stubbornness and an inability to mind her own business.

She was good at it, too. That still surprised her sometimes. In Paris, her connection with Louis had been the key—without their growing intimacy, the truth might have stayed buried with Charles. In Rome, she'd pushed just hard enough to crack Margrit's conscience, to make her choose right over loyalty. People opened up to her. Maybe because she looked harmless, maybe because she listened without judgment, maybe because she had absolutely no authority to make their confessions matter.

Francesco Moretti and Paul Adler would probably laugh at anyone calling her harmless. She'd held a glass shard to Paul's throat, after all. But that was self-defense, not her natural state. Most of the time, she was just Hazel the tourist, Hazel the curious American, Hazel who asked questions because she genuinely wanted to know the answers.

A bus roared past, sending a wave of dirty water toward the sidewalk. Hazel jumped back, barely avoiding a soaking. Dublin was testing her commitment already.

So what was the plan? Murphy had suggested she talk to Zoe's fellow students, dig into the conflicts and secrets that never reached his professorial radar. Riona's comment about Zoe hiding something suggested drama beneath the perfect student exterior. That air kiss definitely pointed toward complications with Cian.

But how would she find him? Or any of the other students, for that matter? She couldn't exactly hang around the university asking random people if they knew anything about the dead girl.

Then she remembered—Emily and she had exchanged numbers after Murphy's lecture. A friendly gesture at the time, but now genuinely useful. Patrick and Emily could help her contact other students, establish a timeline, maybe share whatever gossip she needed to understand Zoe's world.

Hazel pulled out her phone, keeping it under the umbrella's protection. Emily's number stared back at her from the contacts list, saved under "Emily (Trinity)."

Her thumb hovered over the call button. Once she made this call, she'd be committed. No backing out, no catching that flight to Amsterdam, no pretending this wasn't her problem.

But it was already too late for that, wasn't it? She'd seen Murphy's grief, heard Riona's desperation. She'd looked at Zoe O'Brien's body and wondered why, just like in Paris and Rome.

She pressed call.

18

Patrick Keoghan stared at his coffee like it might reveal the secrets of the universe. Or at least explain why they'd had two quizzes before noon—first Murphy, then Byrne.

"Absolute sadists, the lot of them," he muttered, adding another sugar packet to his already-sweet cappuccino.

Emily kicked him gently under the table. "You're just bitter because you didn't do the reading for either class."

"I'm bitter because my brain wasn't designed to function before noon, and they all know it." He stirred aggressively, making the foam swirl into abstract patterns. "Besides, you can't tell me you enjoyed those quizzes."

"I didn't say I enjoyed them. I said I was prepared for them." She took a delicate sip of her own drink—black coffee, because apparently she had no soul. "There's a difference."

"The difference being you actually opened the textbooks while I optimistically assumed they'd ease us in gently on the first day."

"When has any professor here ever eased anyone in gently? Remember first year when Murphy made that girl cry during the very first lecture?"

"In fairness, she did try to argue that homeopathy was legitimate medicine."

"Still." Emily pulled her phone out, probably checking if their afternoon lecturers had posted any surprise reading assignments. "You'd think after a full year you'd learn—"

Patrick's phone buzzed against the table, the caller ID showing Finn's face mid-laugh from last year's Christmas party. He grabbed it quickly.

"Finn, where the hell were you this morning? Missed both lectures."

"Had to help me dad with the shop." Finn's voice sounded breathless, like he'd been running. "Listen, that's not important. I'm at the Biomed and it's absolute chaos here. They're saying Zoe O'Brien is dead."

The words didn't register. Patrick set his cup down carefully, certain he'd misheard. Finn was known for his stories—elaborate half-truths that usually involved him narrowly avoiding disaster through charm or luck. Like the time he'd supposedly talked his way out of a speeding ticket by convincing the guard he was rushing to deliver a kidney. Or when he'd claimed to have accidentally joined a Norwegian black metal band during a stag weekend in Oslo.

"Is this another one of your stories? Like when you said you saw Bono at Tesco?"

"I did see Bono at Tesco! He was buying organic bananas!"

"Finn—"

"I'm serious, Patrick. Dead serious. No joke intended." Something in Finn's voice—an absence of his usual theatrical flair—made Patrick's stomach tighten. "You can come see yourself if you don't believe me. Three Garda cars outside, yellow tape everywhere. It's like something off the telly."

Patrick's eyes widened. Emily noticed immediately, tilting her head in silent question. He held up a finger—one minute.

"What happened?"

"From what I'm hearing, she fell in the bathroom. Hit her head on the tiles or something. Aisling Grant found her—poor girl's probably traumatized for life."

At Aisling's name, Patrick's grip on the phone tightened. Emily's silent questioning became more insistent, her hand reaching across the table.

"Best part is," Finn continued, oblivious to Patrick's reaction, "all the afternoon lectures are cancelled. Silver lining and all that."

Best part? Their classmate was dead and Finn was celebrating free time? Patrick bit back his response. Finn didn't mean it cruelly—he just had the emotional depth of a puddle sometimes.

"Any details? Was it an accident, or…?"

"Nobody knows for sure. Some saying she slipped, others saying the angle's all wrong for that. The guards aren't telling us anything, obviously. Just taking statements from anyone who was in the building."

"Right. Thanks for calling, Finn. Ring me if you hear anything else, yeah?"

"Will do. You coming down to see?"

"Maybe later."

Patrick ended the call, setting the phone face-down on the table. Emily's patience lasted exactly two seconds.

"What's going on? You look like you've seen a ghost."

"That was Finn. He says..." The words felt wrong in his mouth. "He says Zoe O'Brien is dead. Fell in the bathroom at the Biomed. Aisling found her."

Emily's cup rattled against its saucer. "That can't be right. We just saw her in Byrne's lecture. She was answering all those questions, being perfectly Zoe-ish."

"I know."

"She can't just be dead. People don't just die like that."

"Apparently they do."

Emily stared at her coffee, then back at Patrick. "You don't think she just fell, do you?"

"I don't know what to think. Seems a bit convenient, doesn't it?"

"Convenient how?" But Emily was already following his logic. "Oh. Oh no. You think because of Aisling finding her... You think she might have..."

"I don't think anything," Patrick said quickly. "But if someone wanted to hurt Zoe, finding the body gives you a reason for being there, doesn't it?"

"That's mental. Aisling wouldn't... She doesn't even know about Zoe and Cian."

"Are we absolutely certain about that?"

Emily chewed her lip, a habit that emerged when she was thinking hard. "She seemed normal in Byrne's lecture. Sat right next to Cian, held his hand during that boring bit about metabolic pathways."

"Exactly. Would she sit there holding hands with him if she was planning to murder his secret girlfriend the moment class ended?"

"Jesus, Patrick. Murder? We're actually discussing whether one of our classmates murdered another?"

"What else would you call it?"

"An accident. A terrible, random accident." But she didn't sound convinced. "Although... if Hazel saw that kiss Zoe blew at Cian, maybe Aisling saw it too."

"And did what? Followed Zoe to the bathroom and pushed her head into the tiles? Come on, Em. This isn't some crime show."

"You're the one who brought up murder!"

"I'm just saying it's suspicious. The whole thing's suspicious."

They sat in silence for a moment, their coffees cooling forgotten. Around them, the café buzzed with normal life—students complaining about coursework, tourists consulting guidebooks, the hiss of the espresso machine providing soundtrack to it all. None of them knew that just a few hundred meters away, their classmate lay under a white sheet.

"The guards will want to talk to us," Emily said eventually. "All the students who were at the morning lectures, probably."

"Probably."

"What do we tell them? About Cian and Zoe?"

Patrick had been dreading this exact question. They'd kept the secret for three weeks.

"Nothing unless they ask directly. We don't know for certain that it matters."

"Patrick—"

"What? You want to destroy Aisling's world even more? She's just found a dead body. Does she really need to know her boyfriend was cheating on top of that?"

"But if she already knew—"

"You just said she didn't!"

"I said I didn't think she did. There's a difference."

"Is there? Because—"

Emily's phone rang, cutting off what was about to become a proper argument. She glanced at the screen, frowning.

"Who is it?"

"Hazel. The American." She accepted the call before Patrick could voice his sudden unease. "Hello?"

Patrick could only hear Emily's side, but something in her voice—a brittleness that hadn't been there before—made him lean forward.

"Yes, we heard… No, we're fine, just shocked… Of course, we're at Insomnia on Leinster Street… Sure, see you soon."

She ended the call and met Patrick's eyes. "She wants to meet us. Talk about what happened."

"Why?"

"She said she wanted to check if we're okay. Maybe ask a few questions about Zoe."

"Questions?" Patrick's unease blossomed into full suspicion. "Is she some sort of detective?"

"Don't be daft. She's a tourist who came to meet Murphy about her parents."

"A tourist who conveniently shows up right before someone dies?"

"Patrick—"

"I don't like this, Em. Not one bit."

Emily reached across the table, taking his hand. Her fingers were cold from holding her coffee cup. "It's probably nothing. She's just being… American. You know how they are. Over-friendly, getting involved in things that aren't their business."

"That's what worries me."

19

H azel pushed through Insomnia's glass door, wrestling with her umbrella as it fought against closing. The mechanism finally gave in with a snap that made nearby customers glance up from their laptops. She spotted Patrick and Emily immediately—they'd claimed a corner table near the back. They waved, and she returned the gesture, pointing toward the counter to indicate she'd be right there.

The café hummed with afternoon energy, that particular mix of students cramming between classes and tourists seeking refuge from Dublin's weather. The smell of coffee was strong enough to wake the dead, which seemed grimly appropriate given the circumstances. Hazel ordered a ham and cheese sandwich—safe, boring, unlikely to distract her stomach while conducting amateur interrogations—and a large coffee. She'd need the caffeine.

She carried her sandwich and coffee to their table. They'd pushed their empty cups aside, faces wearing matching expressions of shock trying to settle into acceptance.

"Hi," she said, sitting down. "Thanks for meeting me. I'm so sorry about what happened. I know you must be in shock."

"We weren't that close to Zoe," Emily said, her voice carefully neutral. "But she was still our classmate. It's..." She trailed off, apparently unable to find the right word.

"Awful," Patrick supplied. "It's absolutely awful. You see someone every day in lectures, watch them answer questions, complain about the same assignments, and then suddenly they're just... gone."

Hazel unwrapped her sandwich, using the mundane action to ease into harder questions. "Did either of you see Zoe after Byrne's lecture ended?"

They exchanged glances—the first of many, Hazel suspected.

"Not really," Emily said. "Everyone scatters during the break between morning and afternoon classes. It's a full hour, so people have routines."

"What kind of routines?"

"Well, some head to the library," Patrick explained. "The real keen ones, trying to review notes while they're fresh. Others grab lunch in the canteen or head out to places like this." He gestured around the café. "A few probably go back to their flats if they live close enough. Sixty minutes is just enough time to feel like you should do something productive but not quite enough to actually accomplish much."

"We always come here," Emily added. "Can't face afternoon lectures without proper coffee. The stuff they serve in the canteen tastes like someone described coffee to someone who'd never tasted it, then that person tried to make it from memory."

The canteen coffee she'd had earlier had actually been pretty good, but Hazel kept that thought to herself.

"Plus we needed to decompress after the morning's quiz ambush," Patrick said. "My brain was fried."

Hazel took the opening, wanting to establish rapport before diving into harder topics. "How did the second quiz go?"

They answered simultaneously—Emily saying "Not bad" while Patrick declared it "Terrible." The contrast made all three of them laugh, tension breaking for just a moment.

"I studied," Emily explained with mock superiority. "Patrick assumed the professors would show mercy."

"When have any of them ever shown mercy?" Patrick shook his head. "I'm an optimist. It's a character flaw."

"It's endearing," Emily corrected, patting his hand. "Stupid, but endearing."

Hazel steered them back to business, keeping her tone conversational. "I'm curious about what might have happened to Zoe. Do you have any theories? Did she have conflicts with anyone?"

Another shared glance. They were definitely holding something back.

"Well," Emily said slowly, "there was that thing with Maeve Delaney. We told you about that—the fight in the library?"

"But that was months ago," Patrick added quickly. "And I can't imagine Maeve killing someone just to become the top student. That's insane. She's competitive, sure, but she's not a murderer."

"I remember you mentioning that fight," Hazel said. "And I agree—academic rivalry seems like a weak motive for murder. What about Aisling Grant? The girl who found the body?"

The change was immediate. Both of them tensed, shoulders tightening, faces carefully blank. Hazel had definitely hit something important.

"Aisling?" Emily's voice pitched slightly higher. "I can't imagine... She and Zoe barely talked. Why would she have any conflict with Zoe, let alone want to hurt her?"

"Well," Hazel said carefully, "I keep thinking about that kiss Zoe blew to Cian when he was leaving the lecture. It seemed so... intimate. And isn't Aisling Cian's girlfriend?"

Patrick's jaw clenched. Emily twisted her coffee cup in its saucer, the scraping sound loud in the sudden silence.

"Is there something going on between Cian and Zoe?" Hazel asked directly. "Something Aisling might have found out about?"

They looked at each other for a long moment, conducting one of those wordless conversations that couples perfected over time. Hazel waited, letting the silence do her work for her.

Finally, Emily sighed. "The truth's going to come out anyway. The guards will ask questions, people will talk. Better to tell it properly than let rumors twist everything."

"Em—" Patrick started.

"No, she's right to ask. If someone hurt Zoe, keeping secrets won't help find them." Emily turned back to Hazel. "But this stays between us for now, yeah? Until we have to tell the guards?"

"Of course."

Patrick slumped in his chair, clearly unhappy but resigned. "Fine. We'll tell you. But you have to understand, we kept quiet because it wasn't our business. We're not gossips."

"I understand," Hazel said, trying to project trustworthiness. "I'm just trying to piece together what happened."

They exchanged one more look, then Patrick nodded. "Alright then. Here's what we know."

20

Emily Farrell took a sip of her cold coffee, grimacing at the temperature but needing something to do with her hands. Telling this story felt like betrayal, even if the person being betrayed was already dead.

"About three weeks ago," she began, "a group from our program decided to go camping. Someone had the bright idea that we should take advantage of the weather—it was actually warm for once, miracle of miracles—and do some class bonding in the Wicklow Mountains."

"Whose idea was it?" Hazel asked.

"Honestly can't remember," Patrick said. "These things just sort of happen. Someone suggests it in the group chat, others jump on board, and suddenly you're trying to figure out who has a tent."

"It was probably Finn," Emily said. "He's always organizing things. Likes being the social coordinator."

"So who went?"

"About a dozen of us in the end. Cian and Aisling, obviously—they're that couple who do everything together. Zoe came, which was actually surprising. She usually only showed up for the big parties, not smaller trips like this. Said camping would be a good break from the city." Emily paused, remembering. "She seemed different on that trip. More relaxed. Laughed more."

"With good reason, as it turned out," Patrick muttered.

Emily continued, "There were others too. Maeve came for one night but left early—said she couldn't afford to miss a full weekend of studying. Darragh was there, few others from our year. The regulars who show up for these things."

"So what happened?"

Emily glanced around the café, suddenly paranoid about eavesdroppers. But the nearby tables were absorbed in their own dramas—a couple having what looked like a breakup conversation, students complaining about assignment deadlines.

"The second night we were there," she said, lowering her voice, "Patrick and I couldn't sleep. It was too quiet—you know how the country is when you're used to city noise. All those rustling sounds that could be anything from rabbits to axe murderers."

"Very comforting," Patrick added dryly.

"Anyway, we decided to take a walk. Clear our heads, maybe see some stars. Getting back to nature and all that. The moon was nearly full, so we didn't need torches. We headed down to the lake—gorgeous spot during the day, even prettier at night with the mountains reflected in the water."

She paused, remembering how perfect that moment had been before it wasn't. The silver path of moonlight across the water,

Patrick's hand warm in hers, the feeling that they were the only two people in the world.

"We were planning to take some photos," Patrick picked up the story. "Emily had this idea about long exposures with the stars. We were being quiet, trying not to wake anyone at the campsite. But as we got closer to the lake, we heard voices."

"At first we thought someone else had the same idea," Emily said. "But then we recognized them. Zoe and Cian, down by the shore. We were about to call out, maybe invite them to join us for photos, when we realized..."

"They were kissing," Patrick finished. "Not friendly kissing. Proper going-at-it kissing. The kind that's heading somewhere very specific if not interrupted."

Emily felt her face flush at the memory. It had been like stumbling into someone's bedroom uninvited. "We tried to leave quietly. Seemed like the decent thing to do. But Patrick stepped on a branch."

"Sounded like a gunshot in all that quiet," Patrick said. "They jumped apart like they'd been electrocuted. Saw us immediately—nowhere to hide on that path."

"Awkward doesn't begin to describe it," Emily said. "There we all were, staring at each other in the moonlight. Cian with his shirt half off, Zoe trying to fix her hair. And about a hundred meters away, Aisling was sleeping in the tent she shared with Cian."

"What happened then?" Hazel asked.

"What could we do? We all walked back to the tents together, trying to pretend this was normal. Zoe was the first to speak, actually. Very calm, very controlled. Said they'd appreciate our discretion."

"'Appreciate our discretion,'" Patrick quoted. "Like we'd caught them reviewing notes instead of being all over each other by the lake."

"Cian was panicking," Emily remembered. "Kept saying Aisling couldn't find out, that she'd kill him. That it wasn't what it looked like—which was rich, considering what it looked like was pretty bloody obvious."

"Did they explain? Say how long it had been going on?"

"They tried to make it sound spontaneous. Heat of the moment, moonlight madness, that sort of thing. But..."

"But it was too practiced," Patrick said. "The way they moved together, how comfortable they were with each other's bodies. This wasn't their first time."

Emily nodded. "So we promised to keep quiet. What else could we do? It wasn't our relationship, wasn't our business. We went back to our tent, they went to their separate tents, and we all pretended nothing had happened."

"But it kept happening?" Hazel asked.

"Once you know people are having an affair, you see the signs everywhere," Emily said. "Just this past Saturday at that start-of-term party at Whelan's—they arrived separately but kept finding excuses to be in the same conversation. And yesterday when we all met up at the bookstore to get our course materials, they made sure to stand in different queues but I caught them stealing glances at each other every few seconds."

"That air kiss this morning was the most blatant thing yet," Patrick added. "Usually they were more careful. But with Cian being late and Murphy kicking him out..."

"She got careless," Emily finished. "Or maybe she wanted people to know. Who can say what goes through someone's head when they're carrying on like that?"

"Do you think Aisling found out? Could she have confronted Zoe in the bathroom?"

The question they'd been dreading. Emily looked at Patrick, seeing her own uncertainty reflected back.

"I don't think she knew," Emily said finally. "Aisling's not subtle about her emotions. When she's happy, everyone knows. When she's angry, everyone really knows. If she'd found out about Cian and Zoe, we'd have heard the screaming from here."

"Tell me about her temper."

"It's not violent," Patrick said quickly. "Just... explosive. Irish tempers, you know? All sound and fury, then it burns out quick."

"There was that time Cian forgot their anniversary," Emily offered. "Went drinking with the lads instead of taking her to dinner. She tracked him down at the pub and called him every name under the sun. Made quite a scene."

"But they made up the next day. They always do. Cian grovels, buys her something expensive, promises to do better. The cycle continues."

"What about actual violence?" Hazel pressed.

Emily thought about it. "She threw a book at him once in the library. But he ducked, and honestly, he deserved it. He'd been flirting with some girl right in front of her."

"So she's capable of physical anger when pushed?"

"I suppose," Patrick said. "But there's a difference between chucking a book at your cheating boyfriend and murdering his mistress in a bathroom."

"Is there?" Hazel asked quietly. "If you're angry enough?"

The question hung in the air like smoke. Emily found herself thinking about that night at the lake, how peaceful it had been before they'd stumbled into someone else's secret. Now Zoe was dead, and secrets had a way of not staying buried.

"Can you give me contact information?" Hazel asked. "For Aisling, Cian, anyone else who might have insights?"

"Why?" The question came out sharper than Emily intended. "Why do you care so much about this?"

Hazel seemed to really consider the question. "Professor Murphy asked me to help. Zoe was special to him—brilliant, dedicated, everything a professor hopes for in a student. And her mother, Riona... she studied with my parents here at Trinity. Same program, same year. It's like this weird connection through time."

"That's a bit of a stretch," Emily said. "You didn't even know Zoe existed this morning."

"No, but I know what it's like to lose someone suddenly. To have questions that might never get answered. If I can help find the truth about what happened to Zoe, shouldn't I try?"

Emily wanted to argue, to point out that this wasn't Hazel's responsibility or her business. But something in the woman's eyes—determination mixed with genuine compassion—made her reach for her phone instead.

"Fine. I'll give you the numbers. But if this comes back on us somehow..."

"It won't. I'm just going to ask questions, see if anyone noticed anything unusual. The guards will do their job, but sometimes people tell things to strangers they won't tell authorities."

Emily read out numbers while Hazel typed them into her phone. Aisling Grant, Cian Blackburn, Maeve Delaney, Darragh Collins, Finn Morrison. With each name, she felt like she was handing over pieces of their small academic world to an outsider.

"Thank you," Hazel said when she finished. "I know this wasn't easy."

"Just... be careful," Patrick said. "If someone did kill Zoe—and I'm still not convinced anyone did—they're not going to appreciate you poking around."

"I'll be careful." Hazel gathered her things, sandwich barely touched. "I'll let you know if I learn anything useful."

After she left, Emily and Patrick sat in silence, watching sunlight suddenly stream through the windows where rain had been just minutes before. The café carried on around them—orders called out, machines hissing, conversations rising and falling—but it all felt distant, muffled.

"Are we in trouble?" Emily asked eventually. "If Hazel figured out about Cian and Zoe from one air kiss, the guards definitely will. And then they'll want to know who else knew."

"We didn't do anything wrong," Patrick said, but he didn't sound entirely convinced. "Keeping someone's affair secret isn't a crime."

"No, but if Aisling killed Zoe because of that affair, and we knew about it..."

"She didn't kill anyone."

"You keep saying that."

"Because I believe it." He took her hand across the table. "Aisling's got a temper, yeah. But she's not a killer. There's a line between throwing books and taking lives, and she wouldn't cross it."

Emily wanted to believe him. But she kept thinking about Zoe's face that morning, lit up with the joy of knowing the answer to every question Murphy asked. All that brilliance, all that potential, ended on a bathroom floor.

Someone had crossed that line. The only question was who.

"Come on," Patrick said, standing. "Let's head back to halls. Nothing good comes from sitting here overthinking."

Emily let him pull her to her feet, but as they left the café, she couldn't shake the feeling that they'd just set something in motion. Hazel Chase was out there now, armed with names and numbers and the kind of determination that solved murders.

Part of Emily hoped she succeeded.
The other part feared what she might find.

21

Hazel stepped out of Insomnia into unexpected sunshine. After the earlier rain, the light felt like Dublin's apology for its weather-related mood swings. She tilted her face up, letting the warmth hit her skin while she still could—knowing Irish weather, it would probably start hailing in five minutes.

The sidewalk was still wet, puddles reflecting fragments of blue sky like broken mirrors. She sidestepped a particularly large one, noticing how other pedestrians did the same automatic dance around the water. Some things were universal—nobody liked wet socks.

She started walking with no particular destination in mind, just needing movement while her brain processed what Patrick and Emily had told her. The perfect student with perfect answers and perfect pearl earrings had been having an affair with someone else's boyfriend. For three weeks minimum, probably longer.

So much for first impressions.

Hazel passed a flower shop, its window display bursting with color that seemed almost aggressive after the gray morning. A couple emerged carrying a bouquet of sunflowers, the woman laughing at something the man whispered. Normal people living normal lives, buying flowers for normal reasons. Not investigating murders or uncovering secrets or discovering that brilliant students could also be homewreckers.

Though was that fair? Calling Zoe a homewrecker? It took two people to have an affair, and from Patrick's description, Cian had been an enthusiastic participant. Shirt half off by the lake, comfortable with each other's bodies—those weren't the actions of someone being seduced against his will.

A bicycle bell rang behind her, and Hazel stepped aside to let the cyclist pass. The rider wore a suit and tie, briefcase strapped to the back of his bike, pedaling like he was late for something important. Dublin seemed full of these contrasts—modern life crammed into old streets, business suits on bicycles, ancient pubs next to sushi restaurants.

Kind of like Zoe herself. The brilliant student who answered every question also blew secret kisses to her lover. The academic star also snuck away for midnight encounters by mountain lakes. People were never just one thing.

Which made Hazel wonder—what else had Zoe been hiding?

Riona had sensed something. A mother's intuition picking up on distraction, changes in behavior. The affair explained some of that, but did it explain everything? Or were there other secrets, other complications that might have led to Zoe's death?

Because perfect students didn't just kiss other people's boyfriends. They also didn't just slip and fatally crack their skulls on bathroom tiles. Not without help.

Hazel turned down a side street, drawn by the smell of fresh bread from a bakery. The familiar scent made her homesick for Sunrise Bakery, for the simple problems of burnt croissants and temperamental ovens. When had her life gotten so complicated? Four months ago, her biggest worry was whether to add lavender to the Saturday scones. Now she was walking through Dublin, planning to interrogate a woman who'd just found a body.

She needed to talk to Aisling Grant. The girlfriend who'd been blissfully unaware of Cian's extracurricular activities—or had she? Patrick and Emily believed Aisling didn't know, said she wasn't subtle about her emotions. But people could surprise you. Maybe Aisling was better at hiding her feelings than anyone suspected. Maybe she'd known for weeks and had finally snapped.

Finding the body certainly put her at the scene. Classic mystery novel stuff—the killer "discovers" the victim, plays traumatized witness while actually being the perpetrator. Hazel had seen it in at least a dozen crime shows back home, usually while folding laundry and critiquing the detective's methods.

Of course, those were fiction. This was real life, where sometimes people just had terrible luck and walked into bathrooms at exactly the wrong moment.

But Hazel's instincts, honed by two successful murder investigations, said this wasn't about luck. Someone had wanted Zoe dead. Someone had pushed or struck her in that bathroom, left her bleeding on the tiles, then slipped away unseen.

The question was who. And why. And whether Aisling Grant was witness or killer.

Only one way to find out.

Hazel pulled out her phone, staring at the number Emily had given her. What exactly was she supposed to say? "Hi, you don't know me, but I'm an amateur detective from California and I'd like to ask about the dead girl you found?" Yeah, that would go over well.

She'd have to improvise. Make something up. Lie, essentially, which she was getting disturbingly good at. First pretending to be Canadian at the Portal yesterday—God, was that only yesterday?—and now... what? Professor Murphy's assistant? A counselor? A journalist?

The street opened onto a small square with a fountain in the center. Water trickled down worn stone, the sound oddly soothing. Hazel sat on a bench, phone in hand, and dialed the number before she could talk herself out of it.

22

Aisling Grant sat in O'Glennon's pub nursing her second pint of Smithwick's and trying very hard not to think about Zoe O'Brien's head at that unnatural angle. The alcohol wasn't helping as much as she'd hoped. Every time she closed her eyes, there was the bathroom floor, the blood, the absolute stillness where movement should have been.

The pub was mostly empty at this hour—too early for after-work drinkers. Just her, two old men arguing about horse racing at the bar, and a bartender who kept shooting her concerned looks. She probably looked like death warmed over. Felt like it too.

The Gardaí had been thorough. Name, address, student ID number. Where had she been before finding the body? Who had she been with? Did she know the victim well? Any conflicts, arguments, unusual interactions? They'd been polite but persistent, especially when she'd admitted to barely knowing Zoe beyond sharing classes.

"Bit unusual then, wasn't it?" the young Garda had said. "Finding the body of someone you barely knew?"

Like she'd planned it. Like she'd woken up this morning thinking, "Grand day to discover a corpse in the ladies' room." They'd even asked for DNA samples—elimination purposes, they said, perfectly routine. She'd agreed because what else could she do? Refusing would only make her look guilty of something she hadn't done.

Cian was with his GAA lads, had been since the break started. Typical. Any excuse to talk about football and drink with the boys. Not that she wanted his company right now. She couldn't face telling him about finding Zoe, dealing with his questions and probably inappropriate jokes. He'd barely known Zoe either—they never talked in class, never partnered for group work. He wouldn't care beyond the shock value of someone their age dying.

Aisling took another sip, the beer bitter on her tongue. What the hell had happened in that bathroom? Zoe had seemed fine during the morning lectures, answering questions with her usual show-off precision. No signs of illness, no stumbling, nothing to suggest she'd end up dead within the hour.

Someone must have pushed her. But who? And why? Zoe was competitive, sure, maybe even a bit smug about her grades. But that wasn't reason enough to kill someone. Was it?

The old men's argument escalated, something about a horse named Emerald Thunder and whether it was worth a bet. Normal problems. Normal lives. What Aisling wouldn't give to care about horse racing instead of murder suspects.

Because that's what she was now—a suspect. The one who'd found the body, been in the building, had opportunity. Never mind that she'd had no reason to hurt Zoe. Never mind that she'd gone into that bathroom planning nothing more violent than fixing her lipstick.

People would talk. They always did. By tomorrow, rumors would be flying around campus. Aisling Grant, the jealous classmate. Aisling Grant, who couldn't compete academically so she competed physically. Aisling Grant, the killer.

Her phone buzzed. Unknown number, and the country code wasn't Irish. American? Who did she know in America?

Could be the Gardaí using some kind of forwarding system. Better to answer, show she had nothing to hide.

"Hello?"

"Is this Aisling Grant?" The accent was definitely American, female, careful pronunciation like she was thinking about each word.

"Yeah, who's this?"

"My name is Hazel Chase. I'm Professor Murphy's research assistant. He asked me to call and check on you, make sure you're doing okay after... after what happened today."

Murphy had a research assistant? American one? Aisling couldn't remember him mentioning one, but then Murphy barely mentioned anything personal.

"I'm fine," she said automatically. "Don't need checking on."

"I understand. It's just... Professor Murphy is concerned about his students, especially those affected by today's events. He wanted to make sure you had someone to talk to if needed."

"Like I said, I'm fine. Been better, obviously, but I'll survive."

There was a pause on the other end. Then: "I know what it's like. Being the one who finds the body. How everyone looks at you differently after, like you're marked somehow. How the police ask their questions in that way that makes you feel guilty even when you've done nothing wrong."

Aisling straightened. "You've found a body before?"

"Unfortunately, yes. And I became a suspect too, just because I was in the wrong place at the wrong time. It's... not easy. The wondering if people believe you, if they're whispering behind your back."

This stranger understood. Actually understood in a way Cian never would, in a way her friends couldn't.

"Where are you now?" Hazel asked. "If you'd like to talk in person, I could meet you. Sometimes it helps to speak with someone who's been through something similar."

Aisling looked around the pub. She'd come here to be alone, but alone wasn't working. The silence just made the memories louder.

"O'Glennon's," she heard herself say. "Near campus. You know it?"

"I can find it. Give me fifteen minutes?"

"Sure. Yeah. Thanks."

She ended the call, wondering if she'd just made a mistake. But Murphy's assistant had sounded genuine, and god knew Aisling could use someone who understood what she was going through.

Her phone buzzed again. Text message this time, from a hidden number.

Probably spam. She'd been getting more of those lately—special offers, prize notifications, the usual garbage. But she opened it anyway, needing the distraction.

It wasn't spam.

It was a link to some image hosting site. Despite her better judgment, Aisling tapped it.

The photo loaded slowly on her phone's weak signal. Two people kissing, bodies pressed close, hands in each other's hair. The image was grainy, obviously taken from a distance, but the moonlight had caught their faces clearly enough to leave no doubt.

Cian and Zoe.

Aisling stared at the screen, her brain refusing to process what her eyes were seeing. That was definitely Cian—she'd recognize those shoulders anywhere, that stupid way he stood with his weight on one foot. And Zoe's blonde hair glowed in the moonlight, her hand gripping his shirt like she owned him.

It couldn't be real. She'd seen them in the same room dozens of times. They never talked, never paired up for anything, never showed the slightest interest in each other. Sure, she'd caught Cian chatting up girls at parties, but she'd always shut that down quick. That was their dynamic—she kept him in line, he behaved himself. An entire year together, through first-year stress and weekend trips around Ireland.

Her hands shook as she zoomed in on the photo. Maybe it was photoshopped, some sick joke. But the details were too perfect—the way Cian's hair stuck up where Zoe's fingers had messed it, the familiar Celtic knot tattoo on his forearm, the body language that screamed intimate familiarity.

Her pint glass hit the table harder than intended, beer sloshing over the rim.

She was going to kill him.

Actually kill him.

Aisling hit Cian's contact, hands still trembling. The phone rang once, twice—

23

Cian Blackburn was living his best life.

"No way that point should've counted," Niall insisted, gesturing with his chips for emphasis. "He was clearly fouled before he kicked."

"You need your eyes checked," Kevin countered. "Clean score, referee made the right call. Just because your lot lost doesn't mean—"

"My lot? My lot?" Niall's voice rose in mock outrage. "We were robbed, pure and simple. That ref probably had money on the match."

Cian grinned into his pint, letting the familiar rhythm of GAA arguments wash over him. This was what he'd missed during summer—the lads, the banter, the absolute certainty that sports were the most important thing in the world. With everyone scattered to their home counties for the break, Dublin had felt empty without these sessions.

"What do you think, Cian?" Tommy asked. "You saw the match, yeah?"

"I think Niall's full of shite as usual," Cian said, dodging the chip Niall threw at him. "But the ref was definitely dodgy. Remember that penalty in the second half?"

That set them off again, four voices competing to be heard over the pub's background noise. McCarroll's had decent food and better prices than the tourist traps closer to Temple Bar. Plus the bartender knew them, which meant faster service and occasional free pints when the till was over.

"Speaking of dodgy," Kevin said, pointing toward the window. "What's the story with all the Garda cars?"

They all turned to look. A patrol car sped past, lights flashing but no sirens.

"That's the third one in ten minutes," Tommy noted. "Must be something big."

Niall pulled out his phone. "Let me check the group chats, see if anyone knows—ah, here we go. Jaysus."

"What?"

"Message from Eoghan. Says some girl was found dead in the Biomed building. In the bathroom."

The table went quiet. Young people dying unexpectedly always made the news, no matter where it happened.

"Anyone we know?" Kevin asked.

Niall scrolled through his messages. "Zoe O'Brien is the name he's got. And—fucking hell—Aisling Grant found the body."

Cian's pint slipped, beer sloshing onto the table. The names hit him like physical blows. Zoe. Aisling. Dead. Body. The words refused to form a coherent sentence in his head.

"Isn't that your Aisling?" Tommy was asking. "And they're both in your program, right? Biochemistry?"

Cian couldn't answer. His throat had closed up, chest tight like he'd taken a hurling ball to the sternum. Zoe was dead? How was Zoe dead? He'd seen her this morning, watched her blow him that stupid kiss when Murphy kicked him out. She'd been alive and smirking and perfect.

"Cian? You alright, mate?"

He wasn't alright. He was the opposite of alright. His phone sat on the table between them, screen dark, hiding the photos he definitely shouldn't have saved. Zoe wrapped in his sheets. Zoe laughing at something he'd whispered. Zoe meeting him at Phoenix Park on a July evening when Aisling was back in Kilkenny.

"I need some air," he managed, standing abruptly.

"Shite, man," Niall said, genuine concern in his voice. "Your girlfriend finding a body like that. That's rough."

Cian pulled a twenty from his wallet, dropped it on the table. "For my food. I'll text later."

He made it outside before his legs gave out, slumping against the pub's brick wall. The September air felt thin, inadequate. He sucked in deep breaths that didn't seem to reach his lungs.

Zoe was dead. Actually dead. Not playing some elaborate prank, not faking illness to avoid an exam.

His phone buzzed. WhatsApp notifications flooding in. He opened the app with trembling fingers.

The Biochemistry group chat had exploded. RIP messages, crying emojis, questions about what happened. Someone had posted a photo from the end-of-first-year party—Zoe in the center, laughing at something off-camera, surrounded by classmates who were now typing condolences.

She'd worn a red dress to that party. Cian remembered because Aisling had commented on it, said Zoe looked like a film star. He'd agreed without really looking, too focused on keeping his face neutral. Later, when Aisling was chatting with friends, Zoe had cornered him by the drinks table.

"Your girlfriend's got good taste," she'd said, that particular smile playing at her lips.

"In what?"

"Dresses. Boyfriends." She'd let her fingers brush his as she reached for a glass. "Shame she doesn't know how to hold onto them."

That was the night it started. Three months ago, early June, after the end-of-year party when most students had already left for summer. Aisling had gone home to Kilkenny the next morning, but Cian and Zoe had both stayed in Dublin—both living there year-round. Three months of meeting up when Aisling was safely counties away, of deleted texts and careful alibis for the few times Aisling visited Dublin. Of feeling alive in a way he hadn't in years.

And now she was gone.

Some awful part of him—the part that calculated angles and advantages on the football field—felt relief alongside the grief. No one would know now. Patrick and Emily had kept their mouths shut so far, probably would continue to. The secret would die with Zoe.

Christ, what kind of person thought like that? His... whatever she'd been to him... was dead, and he was worried about getting caught?

But he couldn't help it. A year with Aisling meant something. The relationship they'd built, the plans they'd made. He loved her, in his way. Just not enough to stop him from wanting Zoe too.

The physical attraction had been immediate, undeniable. The way Zoe moved, how she bit her lip when concentrating, the confidence that radiated from her like heat. He'd never felt anything like it with Aisling. Comfortable, yes. Safe, absolutely. But not that burning need to touch, to taste, to consume.

Would it have lasted? Probably not. He'd felt the spark cooling already, reality creeping in around the edges. The sneaking around was exhausting. The guilt was worse. And Zoe had started making comments about the future, about possibilities that terrified him.

But she didn't deserve to die. Whatever else she'd been—brilliant, manipulative, irresistible—she'd been twenty years old with decades ahead of her.

Unless...

The thought crept in like cold water. Aisling had found the body. His Aisling, who threw books when angry. Who loved him with a ferocity that sometimes scared him.

What if she'd found out? What if Patrick or Emily had broken their promise? What if she'd confronted Zoe in that bathroom, things had escalated, and...

No. Aisling wore her emotions on the surface. She'd been normal during Byrne's lecture, complaining about the quiz, holding his hand during the boring parts. If she'd known about the affair, everyone in a three-block radius would have known too.

His phone rang. Aisling's photo filled the screen—the two of them at the Galway Christmas market last December, she wrapped in a scarf while he made bunny ears behind her head.

He answered, trying to arrange his voice into something appropriate. "Ais—"

"YOU FUCKING BASTARD!"

The words hit his ear like a physical assault. He jerked the phone away, but her voice carried clear across the distance.

"Aisling, what—"

"Don't you dare play innocent with me, Cian Blackburn. Don't you fucking dare!"

His blood turned to ice water. She knew. Somehow, she knew.

"I can explain—"

"Explain? You've been sleeping with Zoe O'Brien behind my back and you want to EXPLAIN?"

"It's not—how did you—"

"Someone sent me a photo, you cheating piece of shite. You and her, all over each other like animals."

"Where are you?" he asked, already pushing off the wall. "We need to talk about this properly."

"Oh, now you want to talk? Where was talking when you were sticking your tongue down that bitch's throat?"

"Don't call her that. She's dead, for Christ's sake."

"Good! Saves me the trouble of killing her myself!"

The words hung between them, horrible in their honesty. Aisling's breathing came harsh through the phone, fury burning through the connection.

"I didn't mean that," she said after a moment, voice smaller. "I didn't—fuck, Cian, how could you?"

"Where are you?" he repeated. "Please, Ais. Let me come to you. We can sort this out."

"O'Glennon's. And you better be here in five minutes or I'm coming to find you, and trust me, you don't want that."

"I'm coming. Don't leave, okay? I'm coming right now."

She hung up without another word. Cian started running, his trainers slipping on still-wet pavement. His mind raced faster than his feet. Who had sent that photo? When was it taken? What else did they have?

And underneath it all, a thought he couldn't shake: This day had started with Zoe alive and his secret safe. Now she was dead and everything was falling apart.

24

Hazel pushed open the heavy wooden door of O'Glennon's, pausing just inside to let her eyes adjust to the dim interior. The contrast from Dublin's bright afternoon made the pub seem like a cave—all dark wood and amber shadows. The smell of spilled beer and decades of fried food hit her immediately.

She scanned the room, looking for red hair and finding it at the bar. Aisling sat hunched over a pint, looking exactly like someone who'd found a dead body and then been questioned by police. Exhausted, rattled, probably halfway drunk.

Hazel started walking toward her, weaving between empty tables. She was maybe ten feet away when Aisling's head snapped up, face twisting from misery to pure rage in the space of a heartbeat.

"You absolute fucking bastard!"

Hazel froze. What had she done? They'd only spoken on the phone, how could she have—

"A whole year!" Aisling was off her stool now, finger pointing like a loaded weapon. "A whole fucking year of my life!"

But the finger wasn't pointing at Hazel. It was aimed past her, at whoever had just walked through the door behind her. Hazel turned to see Cian Blackburn standing in the entrance, looking like he'd rather face a firing squad than his girlfriend.

Oh. Oh no.

So Aisling had found out about the affair. Just now, from the look of things. Which meant she hadn't known when Zoe died, hadn't had a reason to hurt her. Good for the investigation, bad for Hazel's immediate survival as she found herself directly in the crossfire.

"Ais, please, let me explain—"

"Explain? EXPLAIN?" Aisling's voice climbed octaves. "You want to explain why you've been cheating on me with Zoe bloody O'Brien?"

The old men at the bar turned to watch with the dedication of people who'd just found better entertainment than horse racing. The bartender looked up from polishing glasses, clearly calculating whether to intervene or sell tickets.

"Can we not do this here?" Cian edged into the pub, hands raised like he was approaching a wild animal. Which wasn't far off. "Please, Ais, let's go somewhere private—"

"Oh NOW you want private?" Aisling grabbed her pint glass. Hazel took a strategic step sideways, out of the potential splash zone. "Wasn't very private when you were all over her by the lake, was it? "

"Jesus, Aisling—"

"Don't you dare bring Jesus into this! Even He can't save you now!"

Hazel pressed herself against the nearest pillar. She'd been in the middle of a couple's fight before—Janet and her ex had once had a screaming match in the bakery about his gaming addiction—but this was next level. This was Irish next level, which apparently came with more colorful profanity and threats of violence.

"Was it Patrick and Emily?" Cian asked suddenly. "Did they send you the photo?"

"Patrick and Emily?" Aisling's rage found a new target. "They KNEW? Those lying little—how long?"

"I thought that's how you found out—"

"HOW LONG HAVE THEY KNOWN?"

Cian's face said he'd realized his mistake. "Three weeks?"

"THREE WEEKS?" The pint glass trembled in Aisling's hand. "I'm going to kill them. Actually, no, I'll kill you first because you're right fucking here—"

"Okay, that's enough!" The bartender finally moved, crossing to them in three quick strides. He was built like someone who'd broken up plenty of pub fights, all shoulders and authority. "You're not throwing anything in my establishment. Take it outside or take it down a notch."

"But he—"

"I don't care if he slept with the Pope's mother. No violence in my pub."

Aisling glared but set the glass down. Her hands shook with the effort of not throwing it at Cian's head.

"Now," the bartender continued, "are you going to calm down, or do I need to call the guards?"

"Already talked to them today," Aisling said bitterly. "Found Zoe's body, didn't I? His whore's body. Maybe that's karma."

"Aisling!" Cian looked genuinely shocked. "She's dead!"

"And I'm supposed to care? She was sleeping with my boyfriend!"

"She was a person—"

"She was a homewrecking bitch is what she was!"

One of the old men raised his pint in apparent agreement. This was better than any soap opera.

"Right, you're all leaving," the bartender announced. "Now."

"But I'm meeting someone—" Aisling started.

"I'm here," Hazel said, finally making her presence known. "I'm Hazel. We talked on the phone?"

Both of them turned to stare at her like she'd appeared in a puff of smoke. She gave a small wave, immediately regretting it. Nothing like a casual wave in the middle of relationship armageddon.

"You're the American?" Aisling asked.

"You called an American?" Cian asked at the same time.

"Professor Murphy asked me to check on Aisling," Hazel explained, sticking to her cover story. "Make sure she was okay after… everything."

"Oh, I'm fucking brilliant," Aisling said. "Found a body, found out my boyfriend's a cheating bastard. Living the dream."

The bartender cleared his throat.

"How about we sit?" Hazel suggested quickly, spotting a corner table away from the bar's fascinated audience. "All of us. I have some questions that might help with the Gardaí investigation."

"Questions?" Cian looked suspicious. "What kind of questions?"

"The kind that establish where everyone was when Zoe died. Better to have your stories straight now than scramble later."

It was partly true. Also partly her being nosy, but they didn't need to know that.

25

After some grumbling and death glares, they relocated to the corner table. Hazel made sure to sit between them, a human buffer zone preventing bloodshed. The bartender watched them go with the expression of someone who'd be keeping an eye on that corner.

"Okay," Hazel said. "Let's start simple. Cian, where were you when Zoe died?"

"Why do you need to know that?" Aisling demanded. "So he can establish an alibi for killing his side piece?"

"I didn't kill anyone!"

"Maybe you killed her because she was getting too clingy. Wanted you to leave me—"

"That's not—"

"Or maybe she threatened to tell me herself—"

"ANYWAY," Hazel interrupted loudly, "where were you during the break between lectures?"

Cian took a breath, visibly pulling himself together. "I was at McCarroll's pub with my mates from the GAA club. We met up right after the morning lectures, been there the whole time until Aisling called."

"And they can verify this?"

"Yeah, of course. We were eating, talking about the match. Ask anyone at the pub, they'll remember us. Niall got into an argument with the bartender about whether Ronaldo was overrated."

Hazel turned to Aisling. "And you?"

"After Byrne's lecture, I chatted with Saoirse Kelly and Nuala McCarthy for maybe five minutes. Comparing notes about that stupid quiz." Aisling's voice went mechanical, like she was giving testimony in court. "Then I was heading out to meet my study group at the library. Stopped to use the bathroom on the ground floor."

"And that's when you found her?"

"Yeah. Just... there. On the floor." Aisling stared at her pint. "Blood under her head. Her neck was all wrong. I knew she was dead before I even got close."

"Did you see anyone leaving the area?"

"No. The corridor was empty. But there's another exit from that bathroom, goes to the back stairwell. Someone could've left that way."

Interesting. Hazel filed that detail away for later. "Before finding her, did either of you see where Zoe went after the lecture?"

They both shook their heads.

"She usually went to the library," Cian offered quietly. "She had this specific spot she liked. Said the light was perfect."

Aisling snorted. "Of course you'd know her favorite study spot."

"It's not like that—"

"What's it like then? You were just studying anatomy together?"

"Let's focus," Hazel interrupted before round two could begin. "Aisling, can you tell me exactly how you found out about the affair?"

Aisling pulled out her phone with sharp movements, found the message, and shoved it at Hazel. "Twenty minutes ago. Right before I called this waste of oxygen."

The photo was grainy but damning. Two figures by a lake, moonlight highlighting their embrace. The faces were clear enough despite the distance—definitely Cian, and Zoe's blonde hair was unmistakable even in the low light.

"The number's hidden," Hazel observed. "Any idea who might have sent it?"

"Someone with a conscience, apparently. Shame they waited until she was dead."

"Can you forward this to me? The message and photo?"

Aisling's eyes narrowed. "Why? What's Murphy's assistant need with evidence of my boyfriend's infidelity?"

"Ex-boyfriend," Cian muttered.

"Oh, NOW you accept it's over?" Aisling turned on him. "What gave it away? Me calling you a cheating bastard or threatening to throw a pint at your head?"

"Ais—"

"We're done, Cian. I don't want to see you, talk to you, or breathe the same air as you. Get out."

"We should talk about this when you're calmer—"

"GET. OUT." She grabbed her pint glass again. "Or I swear to God I'll redecorate your face with Smithwick's."

The bartender looked over, eyebrows raised in warning.

Cian stood slowly, clearly wanting to say more but thinking better of it.

"Now leave before I do something we'll both regret," Aisling added.

He left, shoulders hunched, shooting one last look over his shoulder. Aisling maintained her death glare until the door closed behind him.

"Men," she said, slumping back in her chair. "They're all shite."

"Not all of them," Hazel said automatically, thinking of Mike back home. Then wondered why he'd been her go-to example of a good man.

"All of them," Aisling insisted. "Just varying degrees of shite. Cian's just gone from regular shite to supreme shite with extra corn."

That was... vivid.

"I'm sorry this happened to you," Hazel said. "Especially today."

"Yeah, well. Finding out your boyfriend's been cheating really puts finding a dead body in perspective." She laughed bitterly. "Christ, listen to me. Girl's dead and I'm making it about my relationship drama."

"Your anger is understandable."

"Is it though?" Aisling studied her empty glass like it held answers. "I mean, if I'd known before... before she died..."

"What would you have done?"

"Honestly? Gone after him, not her. She didn't owe me anything. He did." She signaled the bartender for another pint. "All those times I've seen him flirt with other girls. Warned them off, established my territory like some kind of jealous shrew. And this whole time he's been..."

"You said you'd forward that message?" Hazel prompted gently.

"Oh. Right." Aisling fumbled with her phone, sent the message. "Why do you need it?"

"Because whoever sent this knew about the affair. Had access to photograph them, knew your number, and chose to reveal it right after Zoe's death." Hazel met her eyes. "That timing isn't coincidence."

"You think... you think whoever sent this killed her?"

"I think they're connected. But this message proves you didn't know about the affair until after Zoe died. That's good for you—removes motive."

"Great. I'm not a murderer. Put it on my CV." The fresh pint arrived and Aisling took a long drink. "So who did kill her?"

"That's what I'm trying to figure out." Hazel studied the forwarded message on her phone. "Whoever took this photo has been sitting on it for three weeks. Why reveal it now?"

"To twist the knife? Make the worst day of my life even worse?"

"Possibly. Or because they knew the affair would come out during the investigation anyway. This way, they controlled how you found out."

Aisling considered that. "So they're either sadistic or strategic."

"Maybe both."

"Fantastic. A clever sadist killed Zoe. That narrows it down to half the biochemistry program."

Despite everything, Hazel found herself liking Aisling. She had a dark humor that probably kept her sane in situations like this.

"You said on the phone you found a body before?" Aisling asked. "What happened?"

"Wrong place, wrong time in Paris. Tourist who stumbled into something I shouldn't have." Hazel kept it vague. "The police questioned me, but I was innocent, just like you. You have nothing to worry about—the truth always comes out."

"Does it though?" Aisling stared into her empty glass. "Because right now I feel like everyone's going to think I killed her out of jealousy."

"Not with that message timestamped after Zoe died. It proves you just found out about the affair." Hazel watched as Aisling's phone buzzed again.

Aisling glanced at the screen and sighed. "Speaking of which, I should go. My mam's been texting nonstop about what happened at Trinity. If I don't ring her soon, she'll drive up from Kilkenny convinced I'm the one who died."

"Will you be okay?"

"I'll be grand. Got a date with a bottle of wine and my flatmate's stash of chocolate. Maybe burn some of Cian's things. Therapeutic, you know?"

Aisling signaled the bartender and pulled out her wallet, leaving enough euros to cover her pints plus tip.

"Thanks for this," Aisling said as they headed for the door. "For listening. For trying to help when everything's gone to shite."

"Take care of yourself," Hazel said.

Aisling pushed open the door, squinting at the afternoon sun, and walked away with her head high despite everything. Hazel watched her go, mind already racing through possibilities.

Someone had taken that photo three weeks ago. Someone had kept it secret until today. Someone had wanted Aisling to suffer.

And someone had killed Zoe O'Brien.

The question was whether it was the same someone.

26

The September sun hit Hazel's face as she stepped out of O'Glennon's, making her squint after the pub's dim interior. Still sunny—miracles never ceased. She'd take it. After the scene she'd just witnessed, a little vitamin D felt like the universe's apology for the day's chaos.

She pulled out her phone, shielding the screen from the glare. That photo of Cian and Zoe by the lake—someone had taken it three weeks ago during the camping trip. Someone who'd been there, watching, waiting. Then sat on it until the perfect moment to detonate Aisling's world.

Emily and Patrick had been on that trip. They'd know who else was there, who might have been creeping around with a camera phone playing paparazzi. Time to make another call and hope she wasn't interrupting anything important. Like studying. Or processing the fact that their classmate was dead.

Emily answered on the third ring. "Hazel? Everything okay?"

"Define okay." Hazel started walking, letting her feet choose the direction while her mind processed. "I met with Aisling. There was a bit of a situation."

"What kind of situation?"

"The kind where she found out about Cian and Zoe's affair right in the middle of a pub."

Silence. Then: "Oh no."

"Oh yes. Complete with screaming, threats of violence, and some truly creative profanity."

"How did she find out? Did you—"

"No, I didn't tell her anything." Hazel sidestepped a woman pushing a stroller, the baby inside wearing sunglasses like a tiny celebrity. "Someone sent her a photo. Cian and Zoe kissing by the lake. From your camping trip three weeks ago."

"What?" Emily's voice pitched higher. "But nobody else was there that night. It was just us and them."

"Cian showed up while she was processing this news. Made the mistake of mentioning that you and Patrick knew about the affair."

A groan came through the phone. "He didn't."

"He did. So fair warning—Aisling's not exactly thrilled with you two right now. Might want to give her some space."

"Patrick!" Emily's voice went distant, obviously calling to her boyfriend. "Patrick, get over here. We have a problem."

Muffled conversation, then Patrick's voice joined the call. "What's this about Aisling?"

Hazel gave him the short version—photo, revelation, pub confrontation, their names being dropped. She left out the more colorful details, like Aisling threatening to redecorate Cian's face with beer.

"Brilliant," Patrick muttered. "Just brilliant. As if today wasn't already a disaster."

"About that photo," Hazel said, turning down a quieter street. A cat watched her from a windowsill, orange fur glowing in the sun. "You're sure nobody else was there when you saw them?"

"Positive," Emily said. "We were the only ones out of our tents. Everyone else was asleep."

"Who else was on that trip?"

"Let me think." Papers rustled in the background. "There was Darragh Collins—he's in our program. Quiet guy, doesn't talk much. Finn Morrison was there too, he organized the whole thing."

"Anyone else?"

"Maeve Delaney came for the first night but left Saturday morning. Said she had to study." A pause. "Actually, that rules her out for the photo. The lake thing happened Saturday night."

"Who else?"

"Saoirse Kelly and Nuala McCarthy from our program. They were sharing a tent. And... oh, Brody Mulligan. He's Finn's flatmate."

"That's everyone?"

"I think so. It wasn't a huge group. Maybe a dozen people total."

"Someone was definitely watching that night," Hazel said. "Hidden in the trees maybe, or further up the path. Close enough to get a clear photo."

"That's properly creepy," Patrick said. "Who sneaks around taking photos of people kissing?"

"Someone who wanted leverage. Or someone who was already suspicious and followed them."

"You think whoever took the photo killed Zoe?" Emily asked.

"I don't know. But the timing's not coincidental. They waited until she was dead to send it."

They talked for a few more minutes, Emily promising to text if she remembered anyone else from the trip. Hazel ended the call and scrolled through the contacts Emily had given her earlier. There they were—most of the names from the camping trip. She could start calling them now, asking questions, trying to figure out who'd been sneaking around with a camera that night.

But exhaustion hit her like a wave. She'd started the day sitting in on a biochemistry lecture, learned about a death at the university, spent time with a grieving professor and the victim's mother, witnessed a relationship exploding in real-time, and now faced a list of potential murder suspects who were also amateur photographers.

Her emotional batteries were drained. The idea of more conversations, more lies to detect, more secrets to uncover—it was too much for one day. Even amateur detectives needed breaks.

Besides, what were the chances anyone would just confess to taking that photo? "Oh yes, I was creeping around in the bushes photographing my classmates' intimate moments, then held onto it for three weeks before anonymously sending it to destroy a relationship. Tea?"

Not likely.

Hazel sighed, pocketing her phone. She'd done enough for one day. Tomorrow she could play detective again, armed with names and suspicions. For now, she just wanted to get back to her B&B and maybe process everything that had happened.

Little did she know that her own relationship drama was about to blindside her, and this time she wouldn't be just an observer.

27

First things first—she needed to get organized. The names swirled in her head like alphabet soup, and she'd never keep them straight without writing everything down. Plus, she'd need to do research for this case—and probably future ones, at the rate she was going. Which meant she needed a computer.

She'd been putting it off, making do with her phone and occasional internet cafes, but three murder investigations had made it clear that some tools were necessities. Time to join the twenty-first century and buy a laptop.

The thought made her unexpectedly happy. Ireland was perfect for this—English-speaking country meant standard QWERTY keyboards. She'd read horror stories on travel forums about trying to type on German keyboards where the Z and Y were swapped, or French ones where the apostrophe was hidden in bizarre places. No thank you. Give her boring, predictable English keyboards any day.

Hazel pulled out her phone again, searching for nearby electronics stores. There—PC World, just a ten-minute walk. Perfect.

The store assaulted her with fluorescent brightness and the smell of new plastic. Rows of laptops gleamed under the harsh lighting, each promising to change her life with superior processing power and graphics cards she'd never use.

"Can I help you?" A young man in a PC World polo materialized at her elbow, name tag reading "Dylan" and face reading "please buy something so my manager stops yelling at me."

"I need a laptop."

Dylan's eyes lit up like she'd said the magic words. "Brilliant! What'll you be using it for? Gaming? Video editing? We've got this new model with sixteen gigs of RAM and—"

"Writing. Research. Maybe Netflix if I'm feeling wild."

His enthusiasm dimmed slightly. "Right. So more of a basic model then."

"Very basic. I don't need it to launch satellites or mine bitcoin or whatever laptops do these days."

That got a smile. "No worries. Over here we've got our everyday range…"

Twenty minutes later, Hazel left with a simple laptop in a bag that seemed excessive for its contents. It had been refreshingly painless—she had money now, could just point at something and buy it without agonizing over the price. The inheritance had its perks.

The sunshine was already failing as she walked back, dark clouds muscling in from the west. Dublin's weather was returning to form—she'd gotten her allocated hour of sun for the day. She picked up her pace, not wanting to christen her new laptop with rain damage five minutes after buying it.

Mrs. O'Neill's desk sat empty when Hazel entered the B&B. Perfect. She liked the woman but didn't need another conversation about her day at Trinity. "Oh yes, met the professor, very interesting. Also there was a murder and I'm investigating it because apparently that's my thing now." That would go over well.

Her room felt like a sanctuary after the day's chaos. Hazel set the laptop bag on the small table by the window and carefully extracted her purchase. The setup process was mercifully simple—choose your language, connect to Wi-Fi, decline seventeen different free trial offers.

She opened a new document on the laptop and started organizing her thoughts. At the top, she typed "CAMPING TRIP ATTENDEES" and listed the names Emily had given her.

First, she focused on who could have taken the photo. Cian and Zoe were obviously out—they were the ones being photographed. Aisling had been sleeping in her tent, unaware of what was happening by the lake. Patrick and Emily seemed unlikely too—they'd discovered Cian and Zoe together, and if they'd taken a photo, why send it anonymously and risk exposing their own knowledge of the affair?

Maeve Delaney had left before the lake incident, so she couldn't have taken the photo. But Hazel made a separate note about her—the academic rivalry with Zoe was worth remembering, even if it wasn't connected to the photograph.

That left several names: Darragh Collins, Finn Morrison, Saoirse Kelly, Nuala McCarthy, Brody Mulligan.

Any of them could have been wandering that night. Could have seen Cian and Zoe heading for the lake, followed out of curiosity or suspicion. Could have hidden in the darkness with their phone, documenting the betrayal.

But why? That was the real question. Why take the photo, and why send it now?

Hazel opened the browser and navigated to the image hosting site from Aisling's message. The photo loaded slowly on the B&B's Wi-Fi, pixels filling in gradually like an old-fashioned TV warming up.

She studied it with fresh eyes. The angle suggested the photographer had been maybe twenty feet away, slightly elevated—standing on a slope or behind some rocks. The image was grainy but not shaky, so they'd held still, probably braced against something.

This wasn't a quick snapshot taken in surprise. This was deliberate documentation.

The upload site gave her nothing useful—no username, no email, no identifying information whatsoever. She'd need serious technical skills to dig deeper, skills she definitely didn't have.

But she knew someone who did.

Mike Santos had worked IT miracles for her before. He'd tracked down Vittoria Rossi in Rome when all she had was a decades-old photo, found Aurora De Angelis in Naples from a years-old news article. If anyone could trace this anonymous upload, it would be him.

Hazel opened WhatsApp on her phone, her thumb hovering over Mike's contact. Their last exchange stared back at her—three weeks old now. She'd asked if they could be friends again after he helped her in Rome. His response had been a single word: *Maybe.*

Not no, but definitely not yes. And she'd meant to follow up, to actually work on rebuilding their friendship, but then there'd been Italian police paperwork and witness statements and planning this Dublin trip and—

Excuses. All excuses.

The truth was uglier: she'd only texted Mike when she needed something. Asked for help in Paris, contacted him again in Rome, and now here she was, about to ask for another favor.

That wasn't how friendship worked. That wasn't how you showed someone you valued them beyond their usefulness. She was treating him like tech support, not like someone who'd been her best friend for over a decade.

But what choice did she have? She needed his help, and he was the only person she could ask.

Hazel started typing, hating herself a little with each word.

28

Hey Mike. I know I said we'd work on being friends again and then disappeared for three weeks. I'm sorry. I'm in Dublin now and somehow managed to stumble into another murder investigation (I know, I know, what are the odds?). I hate that I'm only texting when I need help, but I really do need help. There's an anonymous photo that might be connected to the case. Could you work your magic and find out who uploaded it? I understand if you don't want to. I've been a pretty terrible friend.

    She hit send before she could overthink it more, then set the phone aside. He probably wouldn't even respond today. Might not respond at all. She'd treated him like a convenience, and he had every right to—

    Her phone rang.

The WhatsApp screen showed Mike's name, the profile photo still the one from two years ago—him at his computer desk with about seven monitors behind him, making an exaggerated "hacker" face that he thought was hilarious.

He was calling. Actually calling. They hadn't spoken on the phone since Valentine's Day last year.

Hazel's finger hovered over the accept button. Her heart did something uncomfortable in her chest, like it was trying to escape through her ribs. This was just Mike. Her friend Mike. Former friend Mike. Mike who she'd laughed in the face when he confessed his feelings.

She accepted the call before her courage failed.

"Another murder? Seriously?"

His voice hit her with unexpected force. Same Mike, same slight exasperation mixed with humor, same tone he'd used a thousand times when she'd done something ridiculous. Her throat went tight.

"Hi to you too," she managed.

"Hazel, what the hell? First Paris, then Rome, now Dublin? Are you working your way through European capitals leaving bodies in your wake?"

"They're not my bodies. I just happen to be nearby when people die. Totally different thing."

"Uh-huh. Have you considered that maybe you're cursed?"

"Daily. Hourly, actually." She shifted the phone to her other ear, needing something to do with her hands. "How's the shop?"

"Good. Finally convinced Mr. Peterson that his computer problems would stop if he'd quit downloading every 'free antivirus' program he sees advertised."

"He's still doing that?"

"Every few months like clockwork." A pause, then: "So. Dublin murder. Tell me everything."

Hazel found herself relaxing slightly. This was familiar territory—Mike asking questions, her explaining the increasingly ridiculous situations she found herself in. She gave him the rundown: meeting Professor Murphy about her parents, sitting in on his lecture, learning about Zoe's death, the affair revelation, the anonymous photo.

"Jesus," Mike said when she finished. "And I thought my life was complicated because the shop's newest client insists their computer is possessed."

"Is it?"

"Only by malware. But try explaining that to someone who's convinced their laptop is haunted." He paused. "You know, you always find the most creative ways to need tech support. Remember when you called me at 2 AM because you thought your phone was recording you?"

"It was making weird noises!"

"It was updating."

"See, this is why we're a good team."

The present tense hung between them, heavier than it should have been.

"Were," Hazel corrected softly. "Were a good team."

"Yeah. Were." She could hear him breathing, probably doing that thing where he rubbed the back of his neck when uncomfortable. "This is weird, right? Talking like nothing happened?"

"Super weird."

"But also kind of nice?"

"Also kind of nice," she admitted.

"Look, Hazel, about the friend thing. When you asked if we could be friends again…"

Her stomach clenched. "It's okay if you don't want to. I get it. What I did was—"

"Shitty."

The word hit like cold water. "I was going to say regrettable."

"No, it was shitty. But I was shitty too. Blocking you everywhere, refusing to talk. Very mature of me. And when your grandmother died..." He paused. "I was in Boston for an apprenticeship. Wanted to reach out, but I didn't know how to break that year of silence. Figured you didn't want to hear from me anyway."

"You don't have to explain," Hazel said quietly. "I wouldn't have known what to say to me either. Besides, I laughed in your face when you told me you loved me. I think you get a pass on the maturity thing."

Silence stretched between them, the WhatsApp connection crystal clear across thousands of miles.

"Can we maybe have this conversation when you're not in the middle of solving a murder?" Mike finally said.

"Avoiding difficult emotional conversations is literally my brand."

"I've noticed." But there was humor in it now, the sharp edges worn smooth. "Send me the photo link. I'll see what I can find."

"Really? You'll help?"

"Of course I'll help. That's what friends do, right? Help each other. Even when one of them is apparently a murder magnet who responds to heartfelt confessions with hysterical laughter."

"It wasn't hysterical. Just... regular laughter."

"That's so much better."

"I know you're being sarcastic, but I'm choosing to take it as sincere."

"That's very on-brand for you too." His voice went serious. "Hazel, are you being careful? Three bodies in three cities isn't a coincidence anymore. That's a pattern."

"I'm being careful. Mostly asking questions, taking notes. Very boring detective work."

"Remember that time you thought you were being careful and almost fell off the bakery roof trying to fix the sign?"

"That was different. The ladder was defective."

"The ladder was fine. You just thought you could reach that extra inch without moving it."

"Point taken. I'll be extra careful. No leaning off metaphorical ladders."

"Good." Another pause. "I should probably go. Lunch break's over, and I've got Mrs. Espinoza's laptop waiting for me. Plus that photo won't trace itself."

"Mike?"

"Yeah?"

"Are we okay? Or at least heading toward okay?"

He sighed, and she could picture him perfectly—probably in his apartment, barefoot because he always kicked his shoes off the second he got home, maybe absently straightening something on his counter because he couldn't help tidying when he was thinking.

"I don't know," he said honestly. "But this is better than a year of silence, right?"

"Right."

"Send me that link. And Hazel? Try not to find any more bodies before I text you back."

"No promises. Bodies seem to find me."

"Murder magnet."

"Tech wizard."

"That's actually kind of cool sounding. I might put it on business cards."

The call ended with actual laughter, and Hazel sat staring at her phone like it might explain what just happened. They'd talked. Actually talked, not just exchanged stilted texts about whether she needed his help. It wasn't fixed—she could feel all the broken pieces still grinding against each other—but it was something.

She forwarded the image link with a simple *Thanks* and set the phone aside.

They'd managed an entire conversation without the past rearing its head too badly. Just hints and acknowledgments, dancing around the edges of what had broken them. But now, alone with her thoughts, there was no avoiding it.

She let herself think about it. Really think about it. About Mike and feelings and that disaster of a Valentine's Day that had shattered over a decade of friendship.

29

Valentine's Day

February 14th, last year. The day Hazel Chase laughed in the face of love and lost her best friend.

She'd been elbow-deep in bread dough when Janet burst through the kitchen door, brandishing her phone like a weapon.

"Kyle texted 'sup' with three u's," Janet announced. "That's his Valentine's Day message. Three u's."

Hazel worked the dough harder, fold and press, fold and press. "Maybe he's planning something special for tonight?"

"Oh, he's planning something special alright. Probably a six-pack and asking if I want to watch him play Call of Duty." Janet hopped onto the clean counter, which would have earned anyone else a lecture about health codes. "I swear, three months together and the man still thinks romance is letting me pick which game to watch him play."

"That's... something?"

"It's something pathetic is what it is." Janet watched Hazel work. "What about you? Hot date with your kitchen timer?"

"Actually, Mike invited me to a play tonight. Some rom-com at the town theater."

Janet's eyebrows performed an interpretive dance. "Mike Santos invited you to a romantic comedy on Valentine's Day?"

"It's not like that. We always do movies, this is just a play version." Hazel shaped the dough into loaves with practiced movements. "Besides, better than sitting home while Bridget watches her favorite romantic movie for the hundredth time."

"Sleepless in Seattle?"

"While You Were Sleeping. She says Sandra Bullock reminds her of me, which is concerning since that character lies about being engaged to a coma patient."

They worked in comfortable silence for a few minutes, Hazel finishing tomorrow's prep while Janet texted increasingly aggressive emojis to her boyfriend. The afternoon sun slanted through the windows, casting everything in gold. Just another Valentine's Day at Sunrise Bakery, where the romance came in pastry form.

"Seriously though," Janet said eventually. "Mike taking you to a rom-com tonight? That boy's been carrying a torch for you since high school."

Hazel's hands stilled on the dough. "We're friends. We've always been friends."

"Friends who do everything together. Friends who text each other good morning. Friends where one of them looks at the other like she hung the moon."

"He does not—"

"He does. It's adorable and also painful to watch." Janet slid off the counter. "Just... be careful tonight, okay? Valentine's Day makes people do crazy things. Like confess feelings that have been brewing for fifteen years."

"You're being ridiculous."

But Janet was already heading back to the front, leaving Hazel alone with bread that suddenly seemed very interesting to look at.

Mike called while she was walking home, his voice bright with excitement about the play. Live theater had never been her thing, but Mike loved the immediacy of it, the way actors had to commit without the safety net of multiple takes.

"I'm already here grabbing our tickets," he said. "Fair warning, our seats are pretty far back. Turns out a lot of people had the same idea."

"As long as we can see and hear, I'm good."

"Oh, we'll hear. The lead apparently believes projection means shouting at full volume. I watched part of rehearsal last week."

"And you still want to subject me to this?"

"It's so bad it circles back to entertaining. Plus they're doing this thing with the proposal scene that involves actual doves. What could go wrong?"

Hazel found herself smiling despite the weirdness of Janet's warning rattling around her head. This was just Mike. Just her friend wanting to see a probably terrible play that would give them joke material for weeks.

When she got home, Bridget was in full decoration mode. Paper hearts covered most surfaces, and she'd lit enough candles to constitute a fire hazard.

"Expecting someone?" Hazel asked, setting down her bag.

"The day is for everyone, dear. We all deserve ambiance." Bridget adjusted a particularly crooked heart. "Any plans tonight?"

"Mike invited me to a play at the town theater. That new rom-com they've been advertising."

Bridget's hands paused mid-heart-adjustment. "Michael invited you to a romantic comedy? On Valentine's Day?"

"Why does everyone keep saying it like that?"

"Like what?"

"Like there's some hidden meaning. It's a play. We're friends who enjoy mocking bad entertainment together."

"Of course you are." But Bridget's tone suggested she was humoring a child who still believed in Santa. "What time is this totally platonic friend date?"

"Seven-thirty. And it's not a date."

"Mm-hmm. Well, you should probably wear something nice. For the theater, of course. Nothing to do with it being Valentine's Day and going with a handsome young man who's been in love with you since sophomore year."

"Mike is not—"

"Hazel, sweetheart. I may be old but I'm not blind. That boy looks at you like you're made of sugar and he's been on a diet his whole life."

"That's... a really weird metaphor."

"But accurate." Bridget went back to her decorating. "Wear the green dress. It brings out your eyes."

Hazel escaped to her room before Bridget could start planning their wedding. Everyone was being ridiculous. Mike was her friend. Her best friend. The person who'd taught her to ride a bike after her grandmother gave up. Who'd held her hair back when she got food poisoning from sketchy fair food. Who'd been there for every major moment of her life since fourth grade.

But as she stood in front of her closet, she found herself reaching for the green dress.

The town theater squatted between a hardware store and a fitness center, trying its best to look artistic with a hand-painted sign and string lights that had seen better decades. Mike waited outside, and Hazel's steps faltered when she saw him.

He'd dressed up. Actually dressed up, in dress pants and a button-down shirt she'd never seen before, with a dark jacket over it. His hair was styled with actual product instead of his usual finger-combing method.

"Wow," she said. "You clean up nice. Hot date after the play?"

Something flickered across his face, gone too fast to identify. "Just felt like making an effort. You look great too. Very theatrical."

"Bridget insisted. Apparently you can't wear jeans to town theater without offending the muses or something."

"The muses appreciate your sacrifice."

Inside, the theater looked ready for tonight's performance. She'd been here dozens of times for movies, but seeing the stage set up with painted backdrops and props gave the familiar space a different energy. The smell of dusty curtains mixed with popcorn from the concession stand.

They found their seats just as the lights dimmed. True to Mike's warning, they were far enough back that the actors looked vaguely human-shaped, but the acoustics were surprisingly good.

The play was immediately, gloriously terrible.

The lead actor seemed to be performing for a theater three times this size, projecting every line like he was trying to reach orbiting satellites. His romantic interest had clearly been cast for her enthusiasm rather than ability, substituting volume for emotion at every opportunity.

Mike leaned close during a particularly overwrought declaration of love. "I think he just burst my eardrum."

"Shhh," Hazel whispered back, fighting giggles. "This is art."

"This is assault."

She elbowed him gently, the familiar rhythm of their banter wrapping around her like a warm blanket. This was why she loved—liked—spending time with Mike. Everything was easy, comfortable, right.

The dove scene turned out to be the highlight. The birds, clearly not theater professionals, had their own ideas about blocking. One made a determined beeline for the exit while another decided the lead's hair would make an excellent perch. The actor, to his credit, continued his proposal speech while trying to dislodge the bird without breaking character.

By the time intermission rolled around, Hazel's sides hurt from suppressing laughter.

"I take it back," she said as they escaped to the lobby. "This is the best thing you've ever dragged me to."

"Right? And we still have the whole second act. I heard rumors about a dream sequence with interpretive dance."

"Stop. I can only handle so much joy."

They dissected the first act's highlights while waiting in line for overpriced candy, Mike doing devastating impressions of the lead's delivery that had her clutching his arm for support. Everything felt normal, felt right. Janet and Bridget were being paranoid. This was just them, same as always.

The second act delivered on its promise of interpretive dance, plus a plot twist involving secret twins that made absolutely no sense but was performed with such conviction that Hazel found herself oddly invested.

When the final curtain fell—literally, it actually fell and had to be hastily re-raised for bows—they stumbled out into the February night, still giddy from the spectacle.

"That was..." Hazel searched for words.

"Transcendent? Life-changing? The best worst thing ever?"

"All of the above." She hugged herself against the cold, wishing she'd thought to bring a jacket. The green dress was pretty but not practical for February, even in California. "Thanks for inviting me. Way better than watching Bridget's movie."

"Always happy to provide cultural enrichment." Mike shrugged out of his jacket and draped it over her shoulders before she could protest. "Come on, let's walk. I'm not ready to go home yet."

They wandered down Main Street, still quoting the worst lines at each other. Mike's jacket smelled like his cologne—something woody and warm that she'd been smelling for so many years she associated it with safety.

Central Park opened up before them, not grand like its New York namesake but pretty in its small-town way. String lights wrapped around trees, probably left over from Christmas and repurposed for Valentine's ambiance.

"Hey," Mike said suddenly. "Can we sit for a minute? There's something I want to talk to you about."

"Sure." Hazel followed him to a bench near the fountain, tucking his jacket tighter around herself. "Everything okay? You're not sick or something?"

"No, nothing like that." He sat carefully, leaving more space between them than usual. "I just... I need to say something, and I need you to let me get through it before you respond, okay?"

"Okay..." A flutter of unease started in her stomach. Mike was never this serious. Even at funerals, he found ways to lighten the mood.

He stared at the fountain, where the water trickled quietly in the darkness. The string lights reflected in the ripples, creating fragmentary patterns that shifted and reformed.

"We've been friends for fifteen years," he started. "Best friends. You're the first person I text in the morning and the last one I think about at night. When something good happens, you're who I want to tell. When something bad happens, you're who I want to be with."

The flutter became a full hurricane. This wasn't happening. This couldn't be happening.

"Mike—"

"Please. Let me finish." He turned to face her, and the look in his eyes made her chest tight. "I've been in love with you since we were sixteen. Maybe earlier. I kept thinking it would go away, that I'd meet someone else and these feelings would fade. But they haven't. If anything, they've gotten stronger."

No. No no no no no.

"I know this might change things between us, and that terrifies me. You're the most important person in my life. But I can't keep pretending that being your friend is enough when I want so much more."

He was still talking, something about taking a chance, about Valentine's Day seeming like a sign, but Hazel had stopped processing words. This was Mike. Her Mike. Her friend who was supposed to stay safely in the friend category forever.

She looked at his earnest face, at the hope and fear warring in his expression, and a laugh bubbled up from somewhere deep in her chest.

Not a kind laugh. Not an "oh how sweet" laugh.

A full-bodied, shocked, this-can't-be-real laugh that burst out before she could stop it.

Mike's face went still. Completely, utterly still, like someone had hit pause on his emotions.

The laugh kept coming, fed by panic and disbelief. He had to be joking. This was Mike, who once spent an entire day speaking only in movie quotes. Who'd programmed her computer to randomly play the Jeopardy theme song until she agreed to go to trivia night with him. Who never took anything seriously.

"Good one," she managed between giggles. "You almost had me. The serious face really sells it."

"Hazel." His voice was quiet. Too quiet. "I'm not joking."

The laughter died like someone had thrown water on a fire. She stared at him, at her best friend who suddenly looked like a stranger.

"You're serious."

"Yes."

"You're... in love with me."

"Yes."

"Since high school."

"Yes."

The word hit like a hammer each time. She'd laughed. He'd poured out his heart on Valentine's Day in the park under string lights, and she'd laughed in his face.

"Mike, I—" She scrambled for words, for something to fix this. "I'm so sorry. I didn't mean to laugh. I just wasn't expecting—I mean, you're my best friend."

"I know."

"And I love you, I do, but not..." She gestured helplessly. "Not like that. You're like my brother, my partner in crime, my—"

"I get it." He stood abruptly. "You don't feel the same way."

"Wait." She grabbed his hand. "This doesn't have to change things. We can still be friends. Nothing has to be different."

He looked down at their joined hands with an expression that made her want to take it all back, to rewind the last five minutes and respond differently.

"Everything's different, Hazel." He pulled his hand free gently. "I need some time."

"Mike, please. Don't go. We can talk about this."

But he was already walking away, shoulders hunched against more than just the cold. She sat on the bench in his jacket, watching her best friend disappear into the darkness.

"We can still be friends," she called after him. The words hung in the cold night air, mocking her with their inadequacy.

He didn't turn around.

She should have chased him. Should have run after him, made him talk, fixed it somehow. Instead, she sat on that cold bench for twenty minutes, replaying every interaction they'd ever had through this new lens.

All the times he'd shown up at her house with her favorite Chinese takeout, somehow always knowing when she'd had a rough breakup. The way he'd taught himself to bake just so he could surprise her with homemade cookies on her birthday. How he'd shown up at her door with homemade soup and terrible jokes when she had the flu last year. A thousand tiny moments that suddenly meant something different.

By the time she got home, he'd blocked her on everything. Phone, social media, even the Words with Friends game they'd had going for three years. Complete communication blackout.

She'd gone to his tech shop the next afternoon during her lunch break, his jacket folded carefully in her arms. But only the shop manager, Mr. Rodriguez, was there when she arrived.

"Mike's out on a service call," he'd said. "Computer emergency in Moorpark. But I can take that jacket for him."

She'd left it there, feeling like she was surrendering more than just clothing. When she got back to the bakery, Janet had taken one look at her face and pulled her into a hug.

"Give him time, honey. Don't chase him right now—he needs space to process this."

But time had stretched into weeks, then months. Every attempt to approach him met the same response—complete avoidance, like she'd become invisible.

She'd broken her best friend with laughter. Shattered fifteen years of friendship in the span of a giggle. And the worst part was, she couldn't even blame him. If someone had laughed at her deepest feelings, she'd probably have blocked them too.

She'd handled it badly. Worse than badly. She'd been cruel without meaning to be, careless with someone who deserved so much better.

Mike had offered her his heart, and she'd treated it like a joke.

No wonder he'd needed a year to even consider speaking to her again.

30

Hazel's stomach twisted with another sharp pang, reminding her that emotional crisis was no excuse to skip dinner. She needed to stop dwelling on Valentine's Day disasters. Food first, self-pity later.

The Bank on College Green had been good to her yesterday—might as well stick with what worked.

The restaurant was packed with the after-work crowd, suits mixed with tourists, everyone talking over each other in that universal restaurant din. Hazel squeezed past a group of businessmen discussing quarterly reports and found a small table near the back. No Patrick and Emily to share knowing looks across the table this time. Just her and a menu she'd only seen once before.

The same waiter from yesterday appeared at her elbow. He recognized her too, eyebrows lifting slightly.

"Back again? The chowder must have made an impression."

"Actually, I thought I'd try the fish and chips tonight."

"Excellent choice. Won't be five minutes."

True to his word, the food arrived quickly—a piece of cod the size of a small boat, golden batter glistening under the lights, surrounded by enough chips to feed three people. The first bite confirmed what she'd suspected: The Bank didn't do anything halfway. The fish flaked apart perfectly, the batter light and crispy, not the greasy mess she'd expected.

She ate methodically, phone beside her plate in case Mike texted. He'd said he'd see what he could find, and knowing Mike, that meant diving deep into whatever technical maze was required. Computer stuff was Mike's domain. Hers was apparently finding bodies and making terrible relationship decisions.

She'd just finished the last bite and waved down the waiter for the check when her phone buzzed. After paying and leaving a decent tip, she checked the message from Mike. It was... gibberish. A string of letters and numbers that looked like someone had fallen asleep on their keyboard: *dazzler05boom*.

Before she could type "what does this mean," her phone rang. Mike's name filled the screen.

"Hold on," she said, answering. The restaurant noise swallowed her voice. A woman at the next table shrieked with laughter at something her companion said. "Let me get outside."

The evening air hit her as she pushed through the door, cooler than the afternoon but still pleasant. She turned onto a quieter street, away from the tourist crowds.

"Okay, I can hear you now. What's with the secret code?"

"That's not a code, that's the username." Mike sounded pleased with himself. "Whoever uploaded that photo wasn't exactly a master criminal. They didn't use a burner account or even bother logging out after uploading."

"So dazzler05boom is our photographer?"

"Looks like it. The 05 could be a birth year, which would make them about twenty. Pretty young. The upload originated from a Dublin IP address, probably using a local internet provider."

Hazel turned another corner, finding herself on a narrow street lined with Georgian townhouses. Their colored doors looked muted in the fading light—navy blue becoming almost black, cheerful yellow dulling to mustard.

"This is great, Mike. I mean, I have no idea who dazzler05boom is, but it's better than nothing."

"Happy to help. Though I should probably stop enabling your murder investigation hobby. Normal people collect stamps or learn languages."

"Where's the fun in that?" She stepped around a puddle left from the afternoon rain. "Hey, I meant what I said earlier. About us catching up properly. Next time I call, it won't be because I need tech support."

"Actually..." He paused, and she could hear him doing that thing where he drummed his fingers on his desk when nervous. "Speaking of catching up, there's something I should probably tell you."

"What?"

"I'm seeing someone."

She stopped mid-step. Nearly caused a collision with a man hurrying past.

"Oh."

"Her name's Grace. We met at trivia night—you remember I used to drag you to those? She's a teacher at the elementary school. Third grade."

"Oh," Hazel said again, because apparently that was the only word in her vocabulary now.

"Hazel? You okay? You sound..." He trailed off, but she could fill in the blank. Disappointed. She sounded disappointed, which made no sense whatsoever.

"No, I'm fine. Just surprised. That's great, Mike. Really great." The words came out too fast, too bright. "A teacher, that's perfect."

"It's only been a few weeks. Nothing too serious yet."

Yet. The word lodged in her chest like a splinter.

"Well, I'm happy for you. Really. I should go though—got to figure out who this dazzler person is."

"Hazel—"

"Thanks again for the help. Talk soon!"

She ended the call before he could respond, then stood in the middle of the sidewalk staring at her phone like it had personally betrayed her.

Mike had a girlfriend. Mike was dating someone. Mike had moved on.

Why did that feel like someone had rearranged all the furniture in her life while she wasn't looking?

A couple walked past, hands linked, the man gesturing animatedly while the woman nodded along. They moved in perfect sync, that unconscious choreography of people who knew each other's rhythms. Hazel watched them go, an unfamiliar tightness in her throat.

This was ridiculous. She'd rejected Mike—no, worse than rejected. She'd laughed in his face when he'd confessed feelings he'd carried for years. She had no right to feel... whatever this was. Jealousy?

That didn't make sense. She'd never thought of Mike as anything more than a friend.

Had she?

Janet would have told her if Mike was dating someone. Unless Janet didn't know. Or unless Janet had deliberately not told her, which seemed more likely. Protecting Hazel from news that shouldn't bother her but clearly did.

She started walking again, needing movement to process this. Grace. Third-grade teacher. Met at trivia night—their trivia night, the one she and Mike had dominated every Thursday at the local pub once he'd finally convinced her to try it. They'd been unbeatable at pop culture, decent at science categories, terrible at sports. Now Mike had a new partner. In trivia and in... other things.

The thought of Mike kissing some teacher named Grace made her stomach churn. Which was completely irrational. She wanted Mike to be happy. She wanted him to find someone who could give him what she couldn't. Someone who wouldn't laugh when he opened his heart.

So why did she feel like crying?

Because she'd thought he'd always be there. That was the ugly truth of it. She'd rejected him but somehow expected him to stay frozen in place, available whenever she needed him. For computer help or movie nights or just existing as her safety net. Mike had always been her constant, and now he was someone else's.

"Get it together," she muttered to herself. A woman walking a small dog gave her a concerned look. Great, now she was the crazy American talking to herself on Dublin streets.

This wasn't the time for whatever emotional crisis she was having. A girl was dead. Someone had taken that photo of Cian and Zoe, held onto it, then used it like a weapon. Someone who went by dazzler05boom, which sounded like a username a teenage boy would think was cool and never bother changing.

She needed to focus on that, not on imaginary images of Mike holding hands with a teacher who probably had perfect handwriting and organized everything with sticky notes and had never once laughed at someone's heartfelt confession.

The investigation. That's what mattered now. Not her confused feelings about a friendship she'd destroyed a year ago.

31

Hazel turned another corner, trying to orient herself back toward the B&B. The streets all looked similar in this light—rows of townhouses with their rainbow doors, iron railings, Georgian windows reflecting the darkening sky. She'd been walking without paying attention, too caught up in thoughts of Mike and mysterious usernames.

A narrow alley opened to her right, a shortcut between two larger streets. She could see the lights of shops at the far end, hear the distant rumble of traffic. It would cut several minutes off her walk.

The alley was darker than the main street, buildings blocking most of the dying daylight. Wheelie bins lined one wall, and the smell of rotting garbage mixed with something sour—spilled beer, maybe, or worse. She picked up her pace.

That's when she heard the voices.

"Come on, love. Don't be like that."

"Just want to talk, that's all."

A woman's voice, higher, stressed: "I said no. Please, just leave me alone."

Hazel slowed, peering into the shadows ahead. Three figures stood about thirty feet away. Two men had cornered a young woman against the brick wall, their body language aggressive even from this distance. One swayed slightly—drunk or high or both.

"Heard me, didn't you?" The taller man moved closer to the woman, who pressed herself harder against the wall. "Asked you nicely for some change. Least you can do is answer."

"I don't have any money," the woman said. Even from here, Hazel could hear the fear threading through her voice.

"Bet you do. Bet you've got loads. Share the wealth, yeah?"

The second man laughed, a harsh sound that echoed off the alley walls. "Yeah, share. We're all friends here."

Hazel pulled out her phone, ready to call the Gardaí. Then stopped. By the time they arrived, this could escalate badly. The woman tried to sidestep, but the shorter man blocked her path.

"Hey!" The word left Hazel's mouth before she could think better of it. "Leave her alone."

Both men turned, squinting through the gloom. The taller one—rail-thin, greasy hair hanging in his eyes—smiled in a way that made her skin crawl.

"Look at this, Nick. Another bird wants to play."

Nick, apparently the shorter one, scratched at what might have been a beard or might have been dirt. "American, sounds like. Tourists always have money."

"I said leave her alone." Hazel moved closer, noting details automatically. Both men in their twenties, pupils dilated even in the dim light. Definitely high on something. The tall one kept rubbing his nose—cocaine, probably. Their movements were loose, uncoordinated. Good. Drunk and high meant slower reflexes.

"Or what?" Tall one stepped away from the woman, focusing on this new entertainment. "You'll call the guards? Go ahead. Take them ages to get here."

"Or I'll make you leave." The words came out calmer than she felt. Her self-defense instructor's voice echoed in her memory: *Confidence is your first weapon. Make them think twice.*

Both men laughed. Nick actually bent over, wheezing with mirth.

"You hear that, Danny? She'll make us leave."

Danny—the tall one—studied her with bloodshot eyes. "Tell you what, love. Give us your purse and phone, and we'll call it even. Won't even mess up that pretty face."

"Counter-offer," Hazel said. "You walk away now, and I won't have to hurt you."

That set them off again, but their laughter had an edge now. Danny whispered something to Nick, who nodded and grabbed the cornered woman's arm while Danny advanced on Hazel.

"Stay with her," Danny called over his shoulder. "Make sure she doesn't run. I'll deal with this one."

He rushed at Hazel with the confidence of someone who'd never had a woman fight back. His grab was clumsy, telegraphed from a mile away. She sidestepped, using his momentum against him. Her foot swept his ankle as her hands guided his trajectory straight into the nearest wheelie bin.

The crash was spectacular. Danny went down in a tangle of limbs and garbage bags, something that smelled like rotten fish exploding over his head.

"Danny!" Nick abandoned the woman, charging at Hazel with surprising speed for someone that drunk.

But rage made him sloppy. He threw a wild haymaker that would have missed even if Hazel hadn't ducked. She drove her elbow into his solar plexus, watched him fold like a broken chair. A knee to the face as he went down ensured he'd stay there.

Danny was trying to extract himself from the garbage, cursing creatively. Hazel grabbed a bin lid and brought it down on his head with a satisfying clang. He collapsed back into the refuse, finally still.

The whole thing had taken maybe thirty seconds.

"Are you okay?" Hazel approached the woman slowly, hands visible. No need to spook her after what she'd witnessed.

The woman stepped into better light, and Hazel's breath caught.

Dark hair pulled back in a messy bun. Freckles. The same worn textbooks from this morning's lecture, clutched against her chest like a shield.

Maeve Delaney. Zoe O'Brien's academic rival.

32

"You," Maeve said, eyes wide. "You were at Murphy's lecture this morning. Sitting with Patrick and Emily."

"That's right." Hazel glanced back at the two men, confirming they were both thoroughly unconscious. Danny had managed to wrap himself in what looked like week-old Chinese takeout. "I'm Hazel Chase. Professor Murphy's research assistant."

"I'm Maeve. Maeve Delaney." She looked between Hazel and the fallen men, seemingly unable to process what had just happened. "Where did you learn to do that?"

"Self-defense classes back home. My grandmother insisted." Hazel nudged Nick with her foot. He groaned but didn't wake. "What are you doing in this alley?"

"I was studying at my usual café, The Compound." Maeve adjusted her grip on her textbooks. "I was walking to the Luas stop to get home. This is supposed to be a shortcut."

"Not a great shortcut after dark."

"I've done it dozens of times. Never had a problem before." She stared at Danny, who'd started snoring into his garbage pillow. "Thank you. I don't know what would have happened if you hadn't..."

"Come on." Hazel gestured toward the alley exit. "Let me walk you to the Luas stop. Make sure you get there safely."

Maeve hesitated, clearly torn between accepting help and maintaining independence. "You don't have to—"

"I know I don't have to. But those two might have friends, and you've had enough excitement for one night."

That decided it. Maeve nodded, falling into step beside Hazel as they left the alley. The main street felt impossibly bright and normal after the darkness behind them.

"The Luas stop is just a few blocks this way," Maeve said, pointing. They walked in silence for a moment before she added, "I really should have known better. Walking alone through alleys after dark. My dad would have my head if he knew."

"We all take shortcuts sometimes." Hazel kept her tone casual, but her mind was racing. Here was Zoe's rival, practically dropped in her lap. Time to dig carefully. "Rough day, huh? First everything at the university, now this."

Maeve's expression shifted, becoming harder to read. "You mean Zoe."

"Yeah. I'm sorry. I know you two were in the same program."

"We were." Maeve's voice was carefully neutral. "Shared all our classes."

They passed a chipper, the smell of frying oil making Hazel's stomach remember she'd basically inhaled her dinner. A group of teenagers lounged outside, sharing chips and gossiping.

"I guess there was some competition between you two?" Hazel tried to sound like she was just making conversation. "Patrick mentioned something about you both being top students."

Maeve's laugh was bitter. "Competition implies it was a contest. Zoe won everything without even trying. Perfect memory, perfect understanding, perfect bloody everything."

"That must have been frustrating."

"You have no idea." They paused at a crossing, waiting for the light. "I study ten hours a day. Twelve during exams. I read every supplementary text, do every practice problem, attend every review session. And Zoe? She'd breeze through the material once and ace every test."

The bitterness in her voice was impossible to miss. The light changed, and they crossed with a crowd of evening commuters.

"Patrick also mentioned something about a fight in the library?"

Maeve's shoulders tensed. "That was... stupid. Embarrassing, really. We were both stressed about the Murphy exam. I'd booked the private study room days in advance, but when I got there, Zoe was already set up. Said she'd reserved it too."

"Double booking?"

"That's what the librarian said. But I'd checked the system that morning, and my reservation was gone. Replaced by Zoe's." Maeve's jaw tightened. "She denied doing anything, of course. Said I must have made a mistake. But I know what I saw."

"So you fought?"

"I snapped. Threw her notebooks off the table, called her some names I'm not proud of. She threw her coffee at me—ruined my favorite hoodie. Security had to separate us." The anger drained from her voice, replaced by exhaustion. "My parents were furious. Said I was embarrassing the family, acting like a child."

They turned onto a busier street. The Luas stop was visible ahead, the silver tram pulling away as they watched.

"Where were you during the break?" Hazel asked. "After the morning lectures?"

Maeve gave her a sharp look. "Why?"

"Sorry. Professor Murphy asked me to check on students who might have been affected. You know, make sure everyone's okay."

The lie seemed to satisfy her. "I went straight to The Compound. Been going there since the library incident. Can't stand all the staring and whispering now. The café staff know me, save my usual table."

"Did you happen to see where Zoe went after the lecture?" Hazel kept her tone casual. "I'm just trying to understand the timeline."

Maeve's shoulders stiffened. "No. And I don't keep track of her movements. Why would I?"

The defensive response was telling. Maeve was trying too hard to seem indifferent.

"Just wondering if anyone might have followed her or seemed upset with her." Hazel shifted topics, pulling out her phone like she was checking something. "Actually, this is random, but I saw someone had written 'dazzler05boom' in their notebook during the lecture. Been driving me crazy trying to figure out what it means. You know how those things get stuck in your head?"

Maeve stopped walking. "Whose notebook?"

"I couldn't tell—just caught a glimpse when they were packing up. Why, do you recognize it?"

"That's Darragh Collins. He uses it for everything—email, social media, probably his bloody Netflix account." She studied Hazel with new suspicion. "Weird thing to remember from a lecture."

"I have a weird brain. Ask anyone." The Luas stop was right ahead, another tram already approaching. "Always picking up random details that don't matter."

Maeve clearly didn't buy it, but the tram was pulling up. "This is me."

"Take care of yourself, okay? Maybe avoid dark alleys for a while."

"Yeah." Maeve tapped her card against the validator and climbed aboard, then turned back. "Thanks again. For back there. Not many people would have helped."

The doors closed between them, and Hazel watched the tram pull away. Two thoughts competed for attention in her mind.

First: Darragh Collins was dazzler05boom. He'd taken that photo of Cian and Zoe, sat on it for three weeks, then sent it to Aisling right after Zoe died. Why?

Second: Maeve Delaney was hiding something. The careful way she'd talked about Zoe, the tension when asked about her whereabouts—something didn't fit.

The question was whether that something was connected to Zoe's death, or if Maeve was just another student with secrets.

33

Maeve Delaney stood at her front door, key in hand, trying to summon the energy to go inside. The house looked the same as always—tidy garden, pristine white paint, her mother's lace curtains in every window. Picture perfect from the outside, like an advertisement for suburban contentment.

She could hear the TV through the door. Football, from the sound of it. Which meant her father was in his usual spot on the sofa, beer in hand, shouting at players who couldn't hear him.

The lock turned too loudly. No sneaking in quietly tonight.

"Maeve? Is that you?" Her mother's voice carried from the kitchen, pitched high with worry. "We heard about Zoe O'Brien. Is it true?"

Maeve dropped her bag by the stairs, textbooks thudding against the floor. "Yeah, Mam. It's true."

Her mother appeared in the kitchen doorway, dish towel twisted between her hands. She'd been crying—eyes red, makeup smudged despite her attempts to fix it.

"Such a young girl. Her poor mother. I can't imagine—"

"One less excuse now." Her father's voice cut through the sympathy like a rusty blade. He didn't look away from the match. "Without the O'Brien girl showing you up, maybe you'll finally be top of the class."

"John!" Her mother's protest was automatic but weak. Twenty-three years of marriage had worn down her ability to stand up to him.

"What? It's true. How much are we paying for that fancy degree? And she's been coming second to some girl who probably didn't need to work half as hard."

Maeve felt the familiar burn in her chest. Anger, shame, exhaustion all mixed together. "Zoe's dead. Actually dead. And all you can think about is class rankings?"

He finally looked at her, eyes narrowed. "I'm thinking about return on investment. You want to pay your own fees? Get a job at Tesco, see how far that gets you? No? Then you better make this worth what it's costing me."

"John, please." Her mother touched his shoulder. "Not tonight. Dinner will be ready in ten minutes. Maeve, go get changed."

Maeve grabbed her bag and escaped upstairs, her father's voice following her.

"Just saying what needs saying, Cathy. Girl needs to focus on what matters."

Her bedroom door shut out the worst of it. Maeve dropped her bag, kicked off her shoes, and sat on the edge of her bed. The same bed she'd had since she was twelve, same faded duvet cover because "there's nothing wrong with it, why waste money?"

She pulled out her textbooks, stacking them on her desk in neat rows. Biochemical Analysis, third edition. Molecular Methods in Biology. Advanced Organic Chemistry. Each one represented hours of her life, pages memorized through sheer repetition because understanding didn't come naturally.

That was the difference between her and Zoe. Had been the difference.

Maeve changed into comfortable clothes—worn jeans, Trinity hoodie with a coffee stain she'd given up trying to remove. The mirror showed her what everyone saw: tired eyes, stress-pale skin, the look of someone running on caffeine and determination.

"Maeve! Dinner!"

She trudged back downstairs. The dining table was set with the good plates, like having matching crockery could make up for everything else. Her father had moved from the sofa but brought his beer, foam still clinging to his mustache.

"Smells good, Mam." Maeve took her usual seat, back to the wall where she could see both parents.

Her mother served shepherd's pie, steam rising from the dish. Comfort food, probably meant to soften the day's edges. They ate in relative silence, just the scrape of forks and her father's occasional comments about the match.

"So," he said eventually, pointing his fork at her. "This grant application. When's it due?"

"End of the month."

"And now you've got a real chance at it. No O'Brien girl with her perfect scores and connected mother."

"The grant committee doesn't care about connections." The lie came easily. They both knew Riona O'Brien's position at Liffey Therapeutics would have carried weight.

"Don't be naive. Everything's about connections. But now the playing field's level. You put in the work, you should win. Twenty-five thousand and free PhD placement—that's worth something."

Worth my freedom, Maeve thought but didn't say. Worth not having every meal come with a side of guilt. Worth being able to breathe without asking permission.

"I'll do my best."

"Your best wasn't good enough before. Do better."

Her mother touched his arm again, that small gesture that never accomplished anything. "She works so hard, John. Twelve hours a day sometimes."

"And the O'Brien girl probably did it in six. But she's not a factor anymore, is she?"

The shepherd's pie turned to ash in Maeve's mouth. She pushed peas around her plate, constructing and destroying small mountains.

"May I be excused? I need to study."

"You've hardly eaten," her mother protested.

"Let her go," her father said. "Least she's got her priorities straight."

Maeve cleared her plate, rinsed it in the sink, and escaped back to her room. The textbooks waited on her desk, demanding attention she couldn't give.

She opened Biochemical Analysis to chapter fifteen, the same chapter Zoe had probably skimmed once and understood completely. The words blurred together. Enzyme kinetics, substrate specificity, catalytic mechanisms—concepts that felt like a foreign language no matter how many times she read them.

Her phone buzzed. WhatsApp message from her study group, asking if tomorrow's session was still on. She typed back confirmation, then scrolled through the earlier messages. Lots of "RIP Zoe" posts, crying emojis, people who'd barely spoken to her in life claiming devastation at her death.

Maeve set the phone aside and stared at her textbook. In two weeks, she'd submit her grant application. Without Zoe, she might actually win. Financial independence. The chance to stop chasing academic excellence she'd never achieve, to find something she actually enjoyed.

All it had cost was—

No. She couldn't think about that. Not yet.

The textbook's pages rustled as she turned them, each one representing another hour of work ahead. Downstairs, her father shouted at the TV, her mother clinked dishes in the kitchen, and life went on like nothing had changed.

But everything had changed. The question was whether Maeve could live with it.

She picked up her highlighter, selected a passage about protein folding, and got to work. Because what else was there to do? The grant deadline was coming, her father's expectations pressed down like a weight, and somewhere in Dublin, Riona O'Brien was planning her daughter's funeral.

Maeve highlighted another sentence, then another, filling the page with fluorescent yellow. If she covered enough words, maybe she could cover the memory of what had happened in that bathroom.

Maybe she could pretend she hadn't been there at all.

34

Hazel pushed open her room door and kicked off her shoes, not bothering to place them neatly by the wardrobe. Her mind churned through the evening's revelations—Maeve Delaney hiding something, Darragh Collins being dazzler05boom, Mike dating a third-grade teacher named Grace. The last one shouldn't matter, but it kept circling back like a song stuck on repeat.

She dropped onto the bed fully clothed, the springs creaking under her weight. Tomorrow she'd track down Darragh, figure out why he'd sent that photo, maybe get closer to understanding who killed Zoe O'Brien. But tonight, her brain felt like overcooked pasta—mushy and useless.

Outside, she could hear Dublin settling into its nighttime routine—distant laughter from the pub down the street, a car door slamming, someone dragging a wheeled suitcase over cobblestones.

Her phone buzzed against the nightstand. WhatsApp call from Janet.

"Oh no." The words escaped before she could stop them. This was the last thing she needed right now—Janet in full protective mode, probably ready to lecture her about safety or demand she come home immediately. Janet had that particular talent for calling at the worst possible moments, like she had some kind of emotional radar.

But if she didn't answer, she'd wake up to forty-seven messages tomorrow, each more panicked than the last. Better to get it over with.

She swiped to accept. "Hey Jan—"

"Are you okay? I just saw online about a student dying at Trinity and you were supposed to be there today and I've been freaking out for the last hour trying to decide if I should call because what if you were asleep but what if you weren't and something happened and—"

"Janet. Breathe."

"Don't tell me to breathe when you're apparently surrounded by dead bodies again! This is the third one, Hazel. Third city, third murder. That's not a coincidence anymore, that's a pattern. That's a curse!"

Hazel rolled onto her side, phone pressed to her ear. "I didn't find this body. I wasn't even near it. Well, same building, but different floor, different bathroom, totally different situation."

"Oh, well if it was a different bathroom, then everything's fine." Janet's sarcasm could have stripped paint. "Silly me for worrying that my best friend has become some kind of murder magnet."

"Mike already used that term earlier today, when we talked."

The line went quiet. When Janet spoke again, her voice had shifted from panic to curiosity. "You talked to Mike? Actually talked? Not just texted about computer stuff?"

"Yeah, he called on WhatsApp after I asked for his help with something."

"He called you." Janet drew out each word like she was tasting them. "Mike Santos, who had blocked you on everything—actually picked up a phone and called you on WhatsApp."

"It wasn't that dramatic. I asked for help with some tech stuff, he delivered, we talked for a few minutes." Hazel picked at a loose thread on the duvet, wrapping it around her finger. "He mentioned he's seeing someone. A teacher named Grace."

Silence stretched between them, broken only by what sounded like Janet opening and closing kitchen cabinets on her end.

"Did you know?" Hazel asked.

More cabinet sounds, then a sigh. "I might have seen them together last week. At that coffee place on Ventura Street. You know, the one with the pretentious menu where a latte costs seven dollars?"

"And you didn't tell me?"

"You were dealing with Italian police and conspirators who tried to kill you. Seemed like bad timing to mention your ex-best-friend's new girlfriend."

"He's not my ex-best-friend. We're just..." Hazel searched for the right word. "Complicated."

"Complicated. Right." Janet's tone suggested she had opinions about that. "Why do you sound upset about it? You're supposed to be happy he found someone, right?"

"I'm not upset." The words came out too fast, like a bad poker bluff. "Of course I'm happy for him. Why wouldn't I be? He deserves to be happy. To find someone who won't laugh in his face when he shares his feelings."

"Hazel—"

"I'm fine. Really. It's good that he's moving on. Great, even. Third-grade teacher probably means she's patient and good with immature behavior, which, you know, perfect for dealing with guys."

Janet made a noise that suggested she wasn't buying it, but mercifully changed the subject. "So tell me about this dead student. Are you investigating? Since you asked Mike for help, I'm guessing yes."

Hazel sat up, grateful for the topic shift. The movement made her realize she was still wearing her jacket. She shrugged it off, tossing it toward the chair and missing by a foot. "It's a complete mess. The victim was having an affair with another student's boyfriend, there's academic rivalry, anonymous photos being sent around, lies everywhere. These kids are barely twenty and their drama makes daytime TV look subtle."

"Twenty-year-olds doing reckless things? Shocking. Remember us at that age?"

"You're making it sound like we're ancient. That was five years ago."

"Five years ago we were living the dream, covered in flour at four in the morning, arguing about whether lavender belonged in chocolate chip cookies."

"You're the one who thought it did."

"And I was right. They were our best seller that summer." Janet's smile was audible through the phone. "Mrs. Espinoza still asks about them. But seriously, be careful with these Trinity kids. University students can hide all kinds of secrets."

"When am I not careful?"

"Rome. The apartment. Five conspirators. Glass shard to someone's throat."

"That was self-defense. And this time there's no conspiracy. Pretty sure someone just pushed Zoe in a moment of anger. No grand plots or decade-long revenge schemes."

"Famous last words."

They talked for a few more minutes, Janet filling her in on Fillmore gossip—the Thompsons were getting divorced, surprise to no one; the new coffee shop was already struggling because they didn't understand that small-town California didn't need fifteen varieties of alternative milk; someone had graffitied a surprisingly artistic mural on the old water tower and the town council couldn't decide whether to arrest someone or commission more.

"Oh, and Harold stopped by the bakery yesterday," Janet added. "Wanted to know when you're coming back. I told him you were on a European tour of murder and might be a while."

"You didn't."

"I said you were traveling for family business. He grumbled about needing reliable help and shuffled off. I swear the old man's aged ten years since you left. You know how he gets when he has to actually work the counter himself."

When they finally hung up, Hazel lay back against the pillows, exhaustion pulling at her like gravity. Tomorrow she'd find Darragh Collins, figure out why he'd played paparazzi that night at the lake. Maybe get one step closer to finding Zoe's killer.

But tonight, she just needed sleep. And not to think about Mike Santos holding hands with a teacher named Grace who probably had color-coded lesson plans and had never accidentally burned a sourdough starter.

35

The smell of cooking bacon pulled Hazel from sleep better than any alarm clock. She'd dreamed about chasing someone through Trinity's campus, but the buildings kept rearranging themselves like an architectural Rubik's cube. In the dream, Mike had been there too, explaining that the killer was obviously the person with the worst username while Janet threw cookies at passing students.

She showered quickly, then dressed—jeans, long-sleeved shirt, and grabbed her jacket because Dublin weather had trust issues. A quick swipe of mascara and lip balm was all the effort she could muster. She headed down to the dining room, the stairs creaking in their familiar pattern, third and seventh step loudest, something she'd memorized without meaning to.

Mrs. O'Neill was already bustling around, setting out plates with the efficiency of someone who'd been doing this for decades. Only two other guests occupied tables, both absorbed in their phones and coffee.

"Morning, love." Mrs. O'Neill appeared at her elbow with a pot of tea. "Did you hear about that poor girl at Trinity? Terrible business. And you were just there yesterday meeting your professor friend."

"I heard." Hazel accepted the tea gratefully, its warmth seeping through the delicate china. "Very sad."

"Were you there when it happened? Did you see anything?" Mrs. O'Neill's eyes gleamed with the particular interest of someone who lived for local drama.

"I was in the building, but didn't see or hear anything unusual." True enough, if you didn't count the aftermath.

"Such a young life cut short. They're saying she slipped and fell, but you have to wonder." Mrs. O'Neill leaned closer, dropping her voice to conspiracy levels. "My neighbor's daughter goes to Trinity. Says there's all sorts of gossip about affairs and jealousy. You know how students are."

Hazel made noncommittal noises, focusing on the plate of food that had materialized in front of her. Full Irish breakfast again—apparently Mrs. O'Neill believed in consistency.

"What's your plan for today then? More sightseeing?"

"Something like that."

"Well, the weather should hold. Bit cloudy, but no rain expected until evening. Make sure you see St. Stephen's Green if you haven't already. Lovely this time of year. The swans are particularly charming."

Hazel escaped twenty minutes later, stomach full and mind already working through her approach to Darragh Collins. The morning air carried that particular Dublin smell—part rain, part history, part something indefinable that made her think of old books and fresh starts.

She was halfway to Trinity when her phone rang.

"Good morning," Professor Murphy's voice was tired but steady. "I apologize for not calling yesterday. It was... chaotic. I spent most of the day with Riona, helping her navigate the practical matters. Funeral arrangements, notifying family, all the terrible bureaucracy that death brings."

"How is she?"

"Holding together as well as can be expected. She's a strong woman, but losing a child..." He trailed off, and Hazel could hear him taking a steadying breath. "The funeral director kept asking about Zoe's favorite flowers. Such a small thing, but Riona broke down completely. Said Zoe hated flowers, thought they were a waste of money when they'd just die anyway."

"I'm sorry. That must have been awful."

"It was necessary. Someone had to help, and I've known Riona for over twenty years. But yes, awful is the right word." Another pause. "How's your investigation progressing?"

"It's complicated." Hazel turned onto a quieter street, away from morning traffic. "These students have more drama than a soap opera. Affairs, secrets, rivalries. Everyone's lying about something."

"Students usually are. Though not typically about murder."

"I do have one lead—Darragh Collins."

"Darragh?" Murphy sounded surprised. "Quiet boy, sits in the middle rows. Always wears headphones before class starts. What's his connection?"

"I'd rather confirm some things before I say. What can you tell me about him?"

"Not much, I'm afraid. He completes his assignments on time, scores consistently average. Never causes problems but never stands out either. The kind of student who fades into the background. I probably wouldn't remember his name if he hadn't asked for an extension last term—grandmother's funeral."

"Did she actually die?"

"I certainly hope so, given that he provided a death certificate." A hint of Murphy's dry humor crept through. "Though after forty years of teaching, very few grandmother excuses surprise me anymore."

"Do you know if he has classes this morning?"

She heard papers rustling, probably Murphy checking the schedule. "Let me see... I have all the second years' timetables here. Darragh's group doesn't have any classes until after lunch today. Tuesday mornings are usually light for them—most students use the time for catching up on sleep or assignments. He should be free. You could call him, introduce yourself as my assistant—"

Hazel smiled. "Already played that card with a few students. Might need a different approach with Darragh."

"Ah. Burned that bridge already?"

"More like used it up. Don't worry, I have another idea."

"Well, I'm free this morning—no lectures scheduled. Call me after you speak with him?"

"Will do."

She ended the call and pulled up Darragh's number. The Professor Murphy's assistant angle wouldn't work here—something told her Darragh wasn't the type to respect academic authority. But she had another idea, one that might appeal to someone who'd been sneaking around taking secret photos.

36

Convincing Darragh to meet had been surprisingly easy. The words "private investigator from America" had barely left her mouth before he'd agreed, voice eager with the kind of excitement usually reserved for video game releases or limited edition collectibles.

"Wait, like a real private investigator? Like in films?"

"Something like that," she'd said, letting him fill in whatever dramatic blanks he wanted.

"That's class! Yeah, definitely, I can meet. Where? When?"

They'd settled on meeting near the Campanile—public enough for safety, private enough for honest conversation. The iconic bell tower stood at the center of Trinity's main square, a natural gathering point where two people talking wouldn't draw attention.

While she waited, Hazel pulled up his Facebook on her phone. The profile picture showed a thin guy with the kind of complexion that suggested more time with screens than sunshine. His posts were mostly about games she'd never heard of—something called Warhammer featured heavily—and memes that probably made sense if you were twenty and extremely online.

She recognized him immediately when he approached. Same thin build from his profile picture, mousy brown hair that looked like it hadn't seen a comb in days. He walked like he was trying not to take up space, shoulders hunched, each step apologetic. He wore a hoodie, hands shoved deep in the pockets. His eyes darted around, checking who might be watching, before settling on her.

"Ms. Chase?" His accent reminded her of Sean the taxi driver's, though Darragh's version was fainter, probably softened by a year of university in Dublin.

"Just Hazel is fine. Thanks for meeting me." She shifted into what she thought of as professional mode—serious but approachable, the kind of person you'd trust with secrets. "I want to be clear upfront: I don't work with the Gardaí, and this conversation isn't being recorded."

"Zoe's mam hired you?" He fell into step beside her as they started walking, maintaining careful distance like she might be contagious.

"In a way." Close enough to the truth. "I've already spoken with several students, including Aisling Grant."

His shoulders tightened. "Oh?"

"She told me about the photo she received yesterday. Of Cian and Zoe."

"Right. The photo." His voice went carefully neutral, the kind of tone people used when trying very hard not to react. "Everyone's been talking about it. Cian's been asking around, trying to figure out who sent it."

"The timing's interesting, don't you think? Someone sits on evidence of an affair for three weeks, then sends it right after Zoe dies. Almost like they were waiting for maximum impact."

"I wouldn't know anything about that." The words came out too quickly, tumbling over each other.

Hazel stopped walking, turning to face him directly. "My tech assistant did some digging on that photo. Traced it back to an account with an interesting username. Dazzler05boom. Ring any bells?"

The color drained from his face so fast she worried he might faint. His mouth opened, closed, opened again like a fish gasping for air. She could actually see him cycling through potential lies and discarding each one.

"Look," she said, gentler now. "We can do this the easy way where you tell me what happened, or we can dance around it for an hour while you pretend that's not the username you've used for everything since you were fifteen. But we both know that's your username, so why don't we skip the denials?"

They stood frozen for a moment, other students flowing around them like water around rocks. Finally, Darragh's shoulders slumped in defeat.

"This stays between us?"

"Depends on what you tell me."

He started walking again, faster now, like movement could outdistance consequences. "Fine. Yeah, it was me. I took the photo, I sent it to Aisling. Happy?"

"Not particularly. Why don't you start with why you were taking photos of your classmates kissing?"

"It's not—" He stopped, took a breath. "You'll think I'm pathetic."

"Try me."

Another breath, then the words came in a rush. "I've had a thing for Zoe since first year. Not like creepy stalker stuff, just... she was brilliant, you know? Beautiful and smart and confident. The way she'd bite her lip when concentrating, or how she'd twirl her pen during lectures when she already knew the answer but was letting others try first. Way out of my league, but I couldn't help hoping maybe someday..."

He trailed off, kicking at a loose stone on the path. It skittered away, landing in a puddle with a small splash.

"So you went on the camping trip," Hazel prompted.

"I went to all the social stuff she did. Just trying to be around her, maybe have actual conversations beyond 'did you understand Murphy's lecture?' or 'can I borrow your notes?'" His laugh was bitter, self-deprecating. "Pathetic, right? Like she'd ever notice someone like me."

"Human. What happened that night?"

"Couldn't sleep. Never can when camping—all those weird noises, twigs snapping, things rustling in the bushes. I was lying there, probably around one in the morning, when I heard voices. Whispers, really. Male and female."

They passed a group of students arguing about Nietzsche in the particular way of people who'd just discovered philosophy. Darragh waited until they were out of earshot before continuing.

"Would've ignored it except I recognized her voice. Zoe's. She had this way of laughing, really quiet, like she was trying not to but couldn't help it. So I waited until they moved away from camp, then followed. Found them by the lake, and it was her with Cian Blackburn."

"Who had a girlfriend."

"Exactly. There's Cian, who already has Aisling—who's gorgeous, by the way—and he's also getting with Zoe. Some guys have all the luck." The bitterness was sharp enough to cut glass. "So I took a photo. Thought maybe I could use it somehow."

"Blackmail?"

"No! Jesus, no. Just... I don't know. Evidence, I guess. Proof that perfect Zoe wasn't so perfect. That Cian was a cheating bastard who didn't deserve either of them. I was angry. And hurt. And feeling pretty fucking stupid for thinking I ever had a chance."

"But you didn't send them right away."

"Couldn't figure out how without revealing I'd been creeping around with my phone. Everyone would know it was someone from the trip, start asking questions. 'Hey, why were you wandering around at night taking photos?' Not a great look." He shoved his hands deeper in his pockets. "So I waited, figured I'd send it once term started and we were all back in Dublin. By then there'd be more gossip about other things, less focus on who took the photo. Plus, I kept thinking maybe Cian would come clean on his own, save me the trouble."

They'd reached Fellows' Square with its central green space and benches arranged along the pathways. At the heart of the grass stood a modern sculpture—a twisted metal thing that might have been representing knowledge or might have been a plumbing accident.

Hazel chose an empty bench facing the sculpture and sat, gesturing for him to join her. He perched on the edge like he might need to run at any moment.

"Then Zoe died," she said.

"Then Zoe died." He slumped forward, elbows on knees, staring at the ground between his feet. "I went back to my room during the lunch break, and my roommate came bursting in, all excited like it was gossip instead of someone's life. 'Did you hear about Zoe O'Brien? Dead in the girls' bathroom.' I actually threw up. Made it to the bin, thankfully, but still."

"That must have been awful."

"I thought about deleting the photo. Seemed wrong to expose her secrets now, you know? Let her rest in peace and all that. But then I thought about Cian, how he'd get away with the whole thing. Aisling would never know he'd been cheating on her, and he'd just carry on like nothing happened."

"So you sent it."

"Bought a burner phone with cash from some dodgy shop on Nassau Street, uploaded the photo, sent the link. Thought I was being clever." He laughed again, no humor in it. "Forgot to log out of my account on the image hosting site. Rookie mistake."

Hazel studied him—the hunched shoulders, the inability to meet her eyes, the genuine misery radiating from every line of his body. His hoodie had a small hole near the pocket that he kept worrying with one finger. If he'd loved Zoe, even in his distant, hopeless way, he wouldn't have hurt her.

"I appreciate your honesty," she said finally.

"You won't tell everyone? I mean, I know Aisling will probably figure it out, but the whole university doesn't need to know I'm the creep who takes photos of people."

"I won't gossip about it, but Darragh, this is bigger than campus drama now. The Gardaí have technical specialists. They'll trace that photo eventually. Better to tell them yourself than wait for them to come knocking."

He nodded miserably. "Yeah, I figured. My dad's going to murder me. 'First in the family to go to university and you get yourself arrested.' Brilliant."

"You won't get arrested for taking a photo. Though the Gardaí might have questions about privacy violations."

"There's something else." He looked up finally, eyes red-rimmed. "Something they'd probably want to know more than my pathetic crush."

Hazel's attention sharpened. "What?"

"It's about what I saw. After the lectures yesterday."

37

"I know it sounds creepy," Darragh said, still staring at his hands. "But I couldn't help watching Zoe. Even during lectures, my eyes would just... drift. Like gravity or something. She sat three rows ahead, two seats to the left. Always the same spot."

"What did you see yesterday?"

"After Byrne's lecture ended, everyone was packing up, heading out for the break. I was shoving my stuff in my bag—dropped my pencil case, naturally, scattered pens everywhere because I'm smooth like that—when I noticed Zoe talking to Maeve Delaney."

Hazel kept her expression neutral despite the spike of interest. "That's unusual?"

"Are you joking? After their library fight, they could barely exist in the same room. Made group projects a nightmare because we had to schedule around their mutual hatred. Last term we had to do this presentation, and they literally communicated through other people like we were carrier pigeons."

"What were they talking about?"

"Couldn't hear everything, but I caught bits. Something about research data. Zoe said—and I remember this exactly because it was so weird—'I know what you did with your data. Your results are fake.'"

The words hung between them like a loaded weapon.

"You're sure that's what she said?"

"Positive. Had that tone she used when she knew she was right about something. Made you want to check your work twice just in case. Like when she corrected Professor Murphy about enzyme classification and he actually had to look it up. She was right, obviously."

"What did Maeve say?"

"Couldn't hear her response. She went proper pale though, like someone had dumped ice water on her. Kept shaking her head, but Zoe wasn't having it."

"What happened next?"

"That's the really weird part." Darragh shifted on the bench, his voice dropping lower. "They left together. Same direction, walking maybe two feet apart but definitely together. Maeve looked like she wanted to be anywhere else, but she went. Looked like Zoe was leading, Maeve following."

Hazel's mind raced through possibilities, none of them good. "Which direction?"

"Toward the ground floor. Where the..." He swallowed. "Where the bathrooms are."

The implications settled between them like a stone dropping into still water.

"Did you follow them?"

"God, no. Following Zoe to the lake was bad enough. Following her in broad daylight would've been proper stalker territory." He rubbed his face with both hands. "Should I have? Would she still be alive if I'd—"

"Don't." Hazel's voice came out sharper than intended. "That path leads nowhere good. You couldn't have known."

"But I did know Maeve hated her. Everyone knew. The way she'd stare at Zoe during lectures, especially when Zoe answered another question perfectly. Pure poison in those looks."

"Hating someone and killing them are very different things."

"Are they though?" He looked genuinely curious now, academic almost. "I mean, in the heat of the moment? If Zoe threatened to expose whatever Maeve did, ruin her career before it started?"

The question hung unfinished. Hazel stood, suddenly needing movement. "I don't know what to think yet. But you're right—the Gardaí need to know about this. Both things. The photo and what you saw."

"When should I tell them?"

"Soon. But maybe hold off for just a bit. Let me follow up on some things first."

He nodded, looking younger than his twenty years. Lost. "I really did like her, you know. Never would've hurt her. Used to imagine asking her for coffee, rehearsed it in my head a hundred times. Never worked up the courage."

"I know."

They parted ways at the edge of the square, Darragh shuffling off toward the student accommodations while Hazel pulled out her phone. The morning had grown warmer, sun trying to break through the cloud cover without much success.

Professor Murphy answered on the second ring.

"That was quick. How did it go?"

"Complicated. Darragh saw Zoe and Maeve together after your lecture. Heard Zoe say she knew Maeve's research data was fake."

Silence on the other end, then: "The grant project."

"What grant project?"

"The Brennan-Walsh Memorial Research Fellowship. Twenty-five thousand euros in prize money plus guaranteed PhD placement. Awarded for the best original research conducted over summer holiday. Both Maeve and Zoe were competing for it this year." His voice went thoughtful. "If Zoe discovered Maeve had falsified data..."

"It would end Maeve's academic career."

"At minimum. Research fraud is taken extremely seriously. She'd be expelled, banned from any reputable program. Her name would be mud in the academic community. For someone like Maeve, who's worked so hard to compete with Zoe, it would be devastating."

"Devastating enough to kill for?"

Another pause. She could hear him breathing, probably doing that thing where he polished his glasses while thinking. "I'd like to say no. But pressure does terrible things to people. And Maeve... you can see it in her during lectures. The desperation to excel, the way she tenses up whenever Zoe answers a question. That kind of pressure can break people."

"We need to know what Zoe found. Would she have kept evidence?"

"Almost certainly. Zoe was meticulous about documentation. If she discovered fraud, she'd have proof. Probably digital copies and physical backups, knowing her." He cleared his throat. "Riona asked me yesterday to let her know if there was anything she could do to help find answers."

"You think she'd let us look through Zoe's things?"

"Given the circumstances, yes. She wants the truth more than she wants privacy right now. Shall I call her? We could meet at Pearse Station and take the DART to her house."

Hazel checked the time. Still morning, though it felt like she'd been awake for days. "Let's do it."

"Meet me at Pearse Station in thirty minutes. Platform 1, southbound side. And Hazel? Well done. You're quite good at this."

"Getting people to confess their secrets? It's a gift."

"Or a curse, depending on how you look at it."

She ended the call and stood for a moment, watching students hurry between buildings. Somewhere among them was Maeve Delaney, who'd lied about seeing Zoe yesterday. Who had some secret about her research that Zoe had discovered.

Who might have killed to keep that secret buried.

38

Hazel stood under the railway bridge, listening to the rumble of trains overhead and wondering if she'd somehow wandered into an alternate dimension where DART stations existed in theory but not in practice.

Google Maps insisted she was practically standing on top of Pearse Station. The little blue dot on her phone screen overlapped perfectly with the station marker. Yet all she could see were gray stone walls and absolutely no sign of an entrance.

A train thundered past above her, close enough that she could feel the vibrations through the pavement. So the station definitely existed. The trains were real. But apparently the entrance was playing hide and seek, and winning.

She walked back toward the Biomedical Sciences building for the third time, phone held high like she was trying to summon the entrance through sheer force of GPS signal. The map kept insisting she should turn left at a spot that was clearly just a solid wall. Unless Platform 9¾ had relocated to Dublin, she was out of luck.

Perfect. Here she was, supposedly getting good at this whole amateur detective thing, had actually made real progress on Zoe's case, and now everything ground to a halt because she couldn't find a damn train station entrance.

The thought of calling Professor Murphy crossed her mind. He'd given her clear directions—Pearse Station, Platform 1, southbound side. But calling to admit she couldn't even find the station? That would be like raising her hand in class to ask where the classroom was while already sitting in it.

A student hurried past, earbuds in, backpack bouncing with each step. Hazel swallowed her pride and stepped into his path.

"Excuse me, sorry—where's the entrance to Pearse Station?"

The student pulled out one earbud, looking mildly annoyed at the interruption. "Down there." He pointed past the Biomed building. "Past the next building too, then around the corner. Glass doors, can't miss it."

Can't miss it. Right. Except she'd apparently missed it three times already.

"Thanks."

The student nodded and hurried off, probably late for something important. Hazel followed his directions, walking past the Biomed building, then past another modern structure. Around the corner, exactly where the student had promised, stood a perfectly obvious entrance with "Pearse Station" written on a blue station sign near the door.

She checked her phone. Google Maps now showed her a full block away from where it claimed the station was. What genius in Silicon Valley had decided that accuracy was optional when it came to public transport? Probably someone who'd never tried to navigate a foreign city while solving a murder.

The station interior was all modern efficiency—bright lights, digital displays, the smell of coffee mixing with that particular train station scent of metal and movement. Professor Murphy stood near the ticket machines, checking his watch with the expression of someone who'd been doing mental calculations about tardiness.

"Ah, Hazel." He looked up as she approached. "Five minutes late. If you were my student and this was a lecture, I'm afraid you'd be learning about enzyme kinetics from the hallway."

"Sorry. Couldn't find the entrance. Google Maps kept sending me on a tour of the neighborhood."

His expression softened slightly. "The navigation apps do struggle with our stations. They can tell you where the tracks are but seem mystified by the concept of actually accessing them. First time using the DART?"

"First time finding it, anyway."

He gestured to the ticket machines. "You'll need to purchase a ticket. Select your destination—we're going to Sandymount—then it'll show you the fare. Or I can get it for you if you prefer?"

"I've got it, thanks." Hazel fumbled with the touchscreen, which had that special lag that all public transport machines seemed to share. The machine accepted her coins grudgingly, like it was doing her a personal favor, then spat out a small paper ticket.

They walked to the ticket barriers. Murphy tapped his plastic card against the reader, which beeped and opened smoothly. Hazel fed her ticket into the slot, retrieved it from the other side, and followed him through to the platform.

"I'd have tagged you through as well, but they only allow one person per card," Murphy explained. "Plus you'd need to tag off at Sandymount anyway."

The display showed three minutes until the next southbound train.

"You don't have a car?" she asked, partly to make conversation and partly from genuine curiosity.

"In Dublin? God, no. The traffic alone would drive me to madness. The DART gets me everywhere I need to go—home to Blackrock, into the city center. Thirty-seven years I've been making this commute, never once regretted not dealing with Dublin traffic."

"Thirty-seven years of the same commute?"

"Routine has its comforts. Predictability allows the mind to focus on more important matters."

The train arrived with a wheeze of brakes and the mechanical chime that seemed universal to transit systems. They found seats easily—late morning meant missing both rush hours. The carriage smelled of coffee and rain, with that underlying scent of thousands of daily commutes ground into the fabric.

"I called Riona while waiting for you," Murphy said. "She's agreed to give us access to Zoe's belongings, though she was quite insistent about knowing what we've discovered."

"What did you tell her?"

"That we're following several leads but nothing conclusive yet. True enough, technically." He adjusted his glasses. "She'll want more when we arrive. Grieving parents always do—they need answers like they need air. But we should be careful about what we share."

"Because of Maeve?"

"If Maeve did harm Zoe—and that's still an if—telling Riona could be dangerous. A mother who's just lost her child isn't likely to wait for legal justice. Better to have proof first, then involve the authorities properly."

The train pulled into Lansdowne Road station. A few passengers got off, replaced by a group of tourists consulting a map and arguing about pronunciation. Hazel watched the city slide by outside—Georgian buildings giving way to more modern developments.

"How well do you know Riona?" she asked.

"Not particularly well from her student days—I taught her, of course, but we weren't close. Since Zoe started at Trinity last year, though, Riona and I have been in touch more often. Parent concerns, occasional coffee to discuss Zoe's progress. She's raised that girl alone for the past decade—her ex-husband lives in London now, rarely sees Zoe. Saw Zoe."

The correction hung between them, that shift from present to past tense that marked loss.

Sandymount station was smaller than Pearse, more neighborhood stop than major hub. They exited onto a tree-lined street where houses sat behind neat gardens, everything speaking of comfortable middle-class stability. The walk to Riona's house took them through quiet residential roads, past homes similar to their destination.

"That's it," Murphy said, nodding toward a semi-detached house with a blue door. "Number forty-two."

The garden was well-maintained, roses still blooming despite the September chill. Murphy rang the doorbell, a cheerful electronic chime that seemed inappropriately upbeat given the circumstances.

When Riona opened the door, Hazel had to suppress a small gasp. The transformation from yesterday was shocking. She'd aged years in twenty-four hours—hair unwashed and pulled back carelessly, no makeup to hide the devastation written across her face. Her clothes looked slept in, or more likely not slept in. Grief had carved new lines around her eyes and mouth.

"Cornelius. Hazel." Her voice was hoarse, probably from crying. "Come in, please."

The house interior was exactly what Hazel expected from a successful single mother—tastefully decorated but lived-in, photos covering most surfaces. Zoe at various ages smiled from frames: gap-toothed elementary school portraits, awkward teenage years, recent shots showing the confident young woman from yesterday's lecture.

"Have you learned anything?" Riona asked before they'd even removed their jackets. "Do you know who did this to her?"

"We're following some leads," Hazel said carefully, glancing at Murphy. "But we need to examine Zoe's belongings to put the pieces together properly."

"Of course. Yes." Riona twisted her hands together. "Her room is upstairs. I haven't... I couldn't bring myself to touch anything yet. It's all exactly as she left it yesterday morning."

She led them up carpeted stairs, past more photos documenting a life cut short. Hazel noticed the progression—early photos included a tall man who must be the ex-husband, but he disappeared from the timeline around the time Zoe would have been ten.

Zoe's room was at the end of the hall. Riona paused with her hand on the doorknob.

"She always kept it so neat. Said a cluttered space meant a cluttered mind." Her voice cracked slightly. "I used to tease her about being more organized than me."

The room revealed itself as they entered—walls painted a soft gray, furniture all clean lines and modern simplicity. A desk dominated one wall, textbooks lined up with military precision. The bed was made with hospital corners, throw pillows arranged just so. It looked more like a carefully curated study space than a twenty-year-old's bedroom.

"I'll leave you to it," Riona said, her voice catching slightly. "I can't... being in here too long, with all her things..." She gestured helplessly at the room.

Her phone rang, cutting off whatever she might have said. She glanced at the screen and sighed. "My sister. I should take this—she's been calling all morning."

She answered the phone as she left, already saying, "Yes, Siobhan, I got your messages..."

Murphy waited until her footsteps faded down the stairs before turning to the desk. "Right then. Let's see what secrets Zoe was keeping."

The laptop sat centered on the desk, silver and pristine like everything else in the room. Hazel opened it, unsurprised when a password screen appeared.

"Any ideas?" she asked.

"Let's think logically. She was twenty years old, born in..." He calculated quickly. "2005. Try 2005."

The laptop rejected it with a small shake.

"Too obvious," Hazel said.

Murphy studied the room, gaze lingering on the textbooks. "She was methodical, organized, but not overly sentimental. No posters of bands or films, no obvious hobbies beyond academic work. Try 4321—sometimes the most organized people choose patterns."

The screen shook its rejection again.

"What about 1234?" Hazel suggested.

"Too simple for someone of her intelligence. Although…" He tilted his head. "Try 9876. Reverse order, but still a pattern."

This time, the laptop accepted the code with a pleasant chime. The desktop appeared, as organized as the physical space—folders neatly arranged, wallpaper a simple geometric pattern.

"Excellent deduction," Hazel said.

"Lucky guess." But he looked pleased. "Now, let's see what we can find."

39

The desktop folders were arranged with the same obsessive precision as everything else in Zoe's life. *Academic Work* dominated the left side, sorted by year and subject. *Personal* took up less space on the right, with subfolders labeled *Photos, Music,* and curiously, *Research – Other Students.*

"Should we feel guilty about this?" Hazel asked, cursor hovering over the folders. "Going through her personal files?"

"Guilt is a luxury we can't afford if we want to find the truth about what happened to her." Murphy's tone was pragmatic, but his expression showed he felt the intrusion too. "Start with the academic folders."

Hazel clicked through the files, each one meticulously labeled with date and subject. Essay after essay, all receiving top marks based on the feedback files saved alongside. Lab reports with data so precisely organized it looked like published research. Class notes that read like textbook chapters, every lecture apparently absorbed and restructured into Zoe's own comprehensive understanding.

"This is insane," Hazel muttered. "When did she sleep? There must be hundreds of documents here."

"Look at the timestamps," Murphy pointed out. "Most were created and completed within hours. An essay that would take most students a week, she finished in an evening."

"That's not normal."

"No, but it's not unheard of. True photographic memory combined with exceptional processing speed. I see perhaps one student like this per decade. Your mother was similar, actually—could read a journal article once and quote it verbatim months later."

They moved to the *Research – Other Students* folder. Inside, individual folders bore familiar names: *Aisling Grant, Cian Blackburn, Maeve Delaney*, and at least a dozen others from the biochemistry program.

"What the hell?" Hazel clicked on Aisling's folder. Inside were text documents with dates going back months.

The first file was titled *Observations – October*. Hazel opened it, and they both leaned in to read:

AG shows signs of insecurity despite outward confidence. Constantly checking CB's phone when she thinks no one is watching. Jealousy issues escalating—confronted Sadie Quinn after tutorial for "standing too close" to CB. Academic performance declining, probably due to relationship drama consumption. Prediction: relationship will implode by year end.

"This is..." Hazel searched for words. "Creepy? Calculating?"

"It's data collection," Murphy said slowly. "She was studying them like specimens."

They opened Cian's folder next. His observation file was even more damning:

CB exhibits classic narcissistic tendencies. Requires constant admiration, shows genuine distress when not center of attention. Multiple instances of flirtation with other female students while AG present—testing boundaries? Establishing backup options? Notable: he shows increased interest in any woman who challenges or dismisses him. Prediction: will cheat within six months if presented with someone who initially rejects him.

"Jesus," Hazel breathed. "She predicted the affair."

"Or engineered it," Murphy said quietly. "Look at that last line. She knew exactly what would attract him."

The implication settled over them like a cold blanket. Had Zoe deliberately presented herself as a challenge to Cian, knowing his psychological patterns? The calculated nature of these files suggested someone who saw human behavior as just another system to analyze and manipulate.

They checked several other folders, finding similar clinical observations. Some were benign—study habits, stress responses, academic strengths. Others were more personal, documenting relationship troubles, family conflicts, financial struggles.

"She was building psychological profiles," Murphy said. "Like a behavioral researcher, but without consent or ethics oversight."

"Why would she do this?"

"Knowledge is power. And Zoe clearly enjoyed having power." He rubbed his temples. "I'm starting to think I didn't know my star student at all. Check Maeve's folder. That's what we really need."

Maeve's folder was larger than the others, with files dating back to September of last year. The observation notes started relatively benign—documenting study habits, class participation, test scores. But as time progressed, the tone shifted.

MD growing increasingly desperate. Twelve-hour study sessions now standard. Noticed hand tremors during morning lecture—excessive caffeine? Adderall? Both? Father visited campus last week, publicly berated her for "only" scoring 97% on Murphy's exam. She cried in bathroom after.

Later entries grew darker:

MD's breaking point approaching. Caught her reviewing my discarded draft papers from recycling bin—looking for insights into my methods? Pathetic but also concerning. She needs to accept that some people are simply born with advantages she lacks.

The most recent entry was dated three days ago:

Reviewed MD's research project data. Results too perfect. Statistical analysis too clean. Ran numbers through verification software—definite manipulation. She's falsified at least 30% of results. Document everything, decide how to proceed.

"There's our proof," Murphy said grimly. "Zoe knew about the falsification."

Hazel navigated to a subfolder labeled *Evidence* and found exactly what they expected—copies of Maeve's research data, analysis showing the falsifications, even screenshots of statistical software highlighting the impossibilities in Maeve's numbers.

"She was thorough," Hazel said.

"She was building a case. The question is what she intended to do with it." Murphy pulled out a flash drive from his pocket. "Copy everything in Maeve's folder. We'll need this."

As Hazel transferred the files, she couldn't help feeling unsettled. The Zoe O'Brien who'd answered questions so brilliantly in yesterday's lecture had also been this calculating observer, documenting her classmates' weaknesses like a predator studying prey.

"How did she have time for all this?" Hazel asked. "Full course load, perfect grades, and she was basically running intelligence operations on her classmates?"

Murphy had been thinking the same thing. "Genetics, partly. Riona was brilliant at that age too—not quite at Zoe's level, but close. When you can absorb material instantly, process it completely in one pass, homework that takes others hours takes you minutes. That leaves considerable time for... other pursuits."

"Creepy pursuits."

"Yes." He sighed deeply. "Though I suspect Zoe saw it as practical. Understanding people's patterns, predicting behavior—it's not so different from analyzing molecular interactions. Just applied to human systems instead."

The file transfer completed with a soft chime. Hazel ejected the drive and handed it to Murphy, who pocketed it carefully.

"Should we look through more files?" she asked.

"We have what we need. Zoe discovered Maeve's fraud and documented it thoroughly. That's motive enough for—"

His phone rang, the sudden sound making them both jump. Murphy checked the display and frowned.

"Speak of the devil," he said quietly, showing Hazel the screen. Maeve Delaney calling.

They looked at each other, the weight of what they'd discovered hanging between them. Somewhere downstairs, Riona was still on the phone with her sister, unaware that her daughter's killer might be calling the professor standing in Zoe's perfectly organized room.

Murphy answered on the third ring, his voice carefully neutral. "Miss Delaney?"

40

Maeve woke to the sound of pipes groaning in the walls—the morning symphony of a house that needed repairs they couldn't afford. Her father would blame the builders, the government, anyone but himself for buying a house he could barely maintain.

She lay still, eyes closed, trying to hold onto the blankness of sleep. But consciousness crept in like water through cracks, bringing with it the full weight of yesterday. The bathroom. The questions. The lies that had tumbled from her mouth so easily.

The research data.

Her stomach clenched. She rolled onto her side, pulling the duvet over her head like a child hiding from monsters. But the monsters were in her head now, replaying every moment in crystal clarity.

The shower ran too hot then too cold, the temperature valve another thing that needed fixing. She stood under the erratic spray, mechanically working shampoo through her hair. Her hands moved through the routine—conditioner, body wash, face cleanser—while her mind churned through possibilities, each worse than the last.

What would happen when they found out about the data? When, not if. Because Zoe had known, and Zoe was nothing if not thorough. There would be evidence somewhere. Documentation. Proof.

Her father was already at the kitchen table when she came down, newspaper spread before him like he was holding court. The Irish Times, always the Irish Times, because "real men read real newspapers, not that online shite."

"Morning," she muttered, heading for the kettle.

He didn't look up. "Front page news about that girl from your course. Taking up space that should go to real issues." He turned the page dismissively. "You heading to the library today?"

"Maybe."

She couldn't tell her parents she'd been avoiding the library since that fight with Zoe. That she'd been studying at The Compound café instead, spending money they didn't have on overpriced coffee just to rent a table.

"Maybe?" Now he looked up, studying her over his reading glasses. "The grant application deadline is in two weeks. You should be living in that library."

Her mother, buttering toast at the counter, kept her back turned but Maeve could see the tension in her shoulders.

"When will you finish the research project?" he continued. "Should be wrapping up by now, shouldn't it?"

"Soon."

"Soon." He repeated the word like it tasted bad. "That's what you said last week. And the week before. Meanwhile, we're hemorrhaging money for your education."

"John," her mother said quietly.

"What? She needs to hear this. The grant comes with twenty-five thousand euros in prize money. You know what we could do with that? Pay off the car loan, fix the boiler, maybe even take your mother to see that specialist in Blackrock Clinic she needs."

Maeve gripped her mug harder, watching steam rise from the untouched tea.

"You have all the advantages now," her father continued. "No competition. No excuses. So why isn't your research project finished yet?"

She could tell them. Right now, just open her mouth and let the truth spill out. About the data. About yesterday. About how she'd never be able to apply for the grant because—

"Nothing to say?" Her father folded the newspaper with sharp movements. "Too busy feeling sorry for yourself to think about practical matters?"

"I have to go." She abandoned her untouched tea, grabbed her bag from its hook by the door.

"You haven't eaten," her mother called after her.

"Not hungry."

She escaped before her father could launch into his favorite lecture about wasting food, about children in Africa, about the value of money and how some people didn't appreciate sacrifices made for them.

The morning air hit her lungs like a slap. She walked quickly to the Luas stop, muscle memory carrying her through the familiar route while her mind spiraled through increasingly catastrophic scenarios.

The grant committee discovering her fraud. Expulsion from Trinity. Her name blacklisted from every university in Ireland, maybe Europe. Her father's rage. Her mother's quiet disappointment. The weight of all that wasted money, all those sacrifices thrown away because she'd been desperate enough to cheat.

The tram arrived, already half-full with morning commuters. She found a seat by the window, bag clutched on her lap like armor against the world. The city slid by outside—suburban houses giving way to shops and offices, normal people living normal lives that didn't include academic fraud and dead classmates.

St. Stephen's Green wasn't her usual stop. The Compound was two stops further, her table probably waiting, staff wondering where she was. But the thought of sitting there, surrounded by other students, pretending to study while her world crumbled—she couldn't do it.

The park gates stood open, inviting. She wandered in without any real destination, following paths between expanses of grass and under mature trees. The gray morning light filtered through the leaves, creating muted patterns on the ground.

A bench appeared beside a big pond where swans glided with choreographed grace. She sat, bag at her feet, and watched the birds circle endlessly. Around and around, going nowhere, achieving nothing. She knew the feeling.

What had she been thinking? The question hammered at her skull. Months of work on the grant project, and when the results hadn't matched her hypothesis, when the data showed her theories were wrong, she'd just... changed them. A few numbers here, a graph there, statistical analysis tweaked until everything looked perfect.

Too perfect, as Zoe had noticed.

Because of course Zoe noticed. Zoe who saw everything, understood everything, excelled at everything without even trying. Zoe who'd confronted her yesterday with that satisfied smile, like catching Maeve cheating was just another achievement to add to her collection.

But surpassing Zoe had seemed impossible any other way. How do you compete with someone who absorbed information like a sponge, who could glance at complex equations and understand them instantly? Maeve studied twelve hours a day and still came second. Always second.

Her phone sat heavy in her pocket. She pulled it out, stared at the screen without really seeing it. Her parents had done everything for her education. Loans, extra shifts, no holidays for three years. All so their daughter could be the first in the family with a university degree, a proper career, a future that didn't involve standing behind shop counters or cleaning other people's houses.

The pressure of it crushed her chest, made breathing feel like work. Every meal at home came seasoned with guilt. Every purchase questioned, every expense justified. And through it all, her father's voice: *"Better be worth it."*

But it wasn't worth it if she couldn't even win honestly. If the only way to beat Zoe was to cheat, and she'd been caught anyway, then what was the point? What was any of it for?

Maybe she should tell someone. Murphy would be disappointed but fair. He'd probably make her withdraw from the grant competition, might insist on academic probation, but she wouldn't be expelled. Probably. Unless what happened yesterday changed things. Unless—

No. She couldn't think about yesterday. Not yet.

But Murphy had always been kind, in his stern way. He'd stayed after class once to explain a concept she'd struggled with, had quietly extended a deadline when her mother was hospitalized. He might understand about the pressure, about what it felt like to always come second.

Before she could talk herself out of it, she found his number in her phone. He'd given it to all his students at the start of their first year—"For genuine academic emergencies only, this is not tech support for your laptop."

He answered on the third ring, voice careful. "Miss Delaney?"

"Professor Murphy, I'm sorry to bother you." The words tumbled out too fast. "I know this is inappropriate, but I need to talk to you. About the grant project. And about... about Zoe."

Silence on the other end, long enough that she wondered if the call had dropped. Then: "Are you alright, Maeve?"

The unexpected concern in his voice nearly broke her. When was the last time someone had asked if she was alright and actually wanted to know the answer?

"No," she admitted. "I'm not. I'm at St. Stephen's Green, but I can meet you anywhere. It's important. I need to tell someone the truth before—" She stopped, swallowed. "I just need to tell someone."

"I can come there," he said after another pause. "I have my research assistant with me—Miss Chase. Would you be comfortable with her presence?"

Hazel Chase. The American woman who'd appeared from nowhere yesterday and saved her from those men. Who'd asked her about seeing Zoe after lectures. Who'd probably known Maeve was lying.

"Actually, that's good," Maeve said. "I lied to her yesterday. She should hear this too."

"Where exactly are you?"

"By the pond. Northwest corner. There are swans."

"We'll be there soon. Maeve?" He paused. "Don't do anything rash. Whatever this is about, we can sort it out."

She almost laughed. Sort it out. Like this was a scheduling conflict or a missed assignment. But she just said, "I'll wait here."

The call ended, leaving her alone with the swans and the weight of truth she was about to spill. Around the park, life continued—joggers on their morning routes, dog walkers letting their dogs sniff every tree, tourists taking photos of swans.

Normal life, which might never be hers again after this conversation.

But at least the crushing weight in her chest had eased slightly. She'd made a decision. Whatever came next, at least she wouldn't be carrying secrets anymore. That had to count for something.

Even if it counted for everything else falling apart.

41

The walk from Pearse station to St. Stephen's Green took fifteen minutes, during which Hazel brought Murphy up to speed about her previous encounter with Maeve. The story of the alley confrontation made his eyebrows climb steadily higher.

"You took on two men by yourself?"

"They were high as kites. Probably couldn't have fought their way out of a paper bag." She stepped around a puddle from last night's rain. "The weird part was Maeve lying about seeing Zoe after the morning lectures. She definitely had something to hide."

"And now she wants to tell us about it." Murphy's tone was thoughtful. "The timing is suggestive. The day after Zoe's death, suddenly overwhelmed by guilt?"

"You think she killed her?"

"I think we should listen carefully to what she says. And what she doesn't say."

St. Stephen's Green bustled with late morning activity. Office workers on early lunch breaks, mothers pushing strollers, tourists clutching guidebooks and looking bewildered by Dublin's refusal to match their expectations of perpetual rain. The park was one of those city oases that made urban life bearable—formal enough to feel designed, wild enough to feel natural.

They found Maeve exactly where she'd said, on a bench facing the pond where a pair of swans conducted their elegant patrol. She looked smaller than yesterday, somehow. Deflated. Her hair was pulled back in a messy bun, dark strands escaping around her face. She wore the same jeans and gray jumper from yesterday—whether she'd slept in them or just couldn't face choosing different clothes, Hazel couldn't tell.

She stood as they approached, hands twisting together in a nervous gesture that made her seem more vulnerable.

"Professor Murphy. Miss Chase. Thank you for coming."

She sat back down, and they joined her on either side, the bench creaking slightly under their combined weight. This close, Hazel could see the evidence of tears—puffy eyes, reddened nose, that particular exhaustion that came from crying yourself empty.

"You said you needed to tell us something," Murphy prompted gently when the silence stretched too long.

Maeve nodded, still staring at the swans. "I don't know where to start."

"The beginning is usually helpful," Hazel suggested.

"Right. The beginning." She took a shaky breath. "My family isn't... we're not like most Trinity students. No money for private schools or tutors or gap years in Australia. My dad works construction when he can get it. Mam does home care for elderly people.

Getting into Trinity, especially biochemistry—it was like winning the lottery for them."

Her voice dropped to barely above a whisper. "Do you know what it's like, being the first in your family to go to university? Everyone watching, everyone expecting you to make it worth all their sacrifices?"

Neither Murphy nor Hazel answered. This wasn't a question that needed responses.

"Every euro they spend on my education is a euro they don't have for other things. New clothes, car repairs, a holiday they haven't taken in three years. And they never let me forget it. Not cruel, just... constant. Little reminders. 'Hope you're studying hard, considering what this costs.' 'Your cousin Eddie is making good money at Tesco, no fancy degree needed.' That sort of thing."

A jogger passed, footsteps rhythmic on the path. Maeve waited until he was gone before continuing.

"First year started okay. Hard, but I managed. Good grades, not the best but respectable. But from the very beginning, there was Zoe O'Brien, who made everything look effortless. Perfect scores without trying. Answering questions before the rest of us even understood them. It was like competing against a computer."

"She was gifted," Murphy acknowledged. "But that wasn't your fault."

"Tell that to my father." Bitterness crept into Maeve's tone. "Second place isn't good enough. Second place doesn't justify the loans, the sacrifices, the constant penny-pinching. He actually asked once if I was too stupid for university. Maybe I should quit, get a real job, stop wasting their money on a degree I couldn't excel at."

Hazel felt an unexpected surge of sympathy. Her own path had been simpler—straight from high school to Sunrise Bakery, no expectations beyond making decent pastries. The pressure Maeve described sounded suffocating.

"The grant seemed like a solution," Maeve continued. "Twenty-five thousand euros. Enough to pay off some loans, maybe even have breathing room. And the PhD placement would mean a real career, eventually. But winning meant surpassing Zoe, and surpassing Zoe meant doing something extraordinary."

She finally looked up from the swans, meeting Murphy's gaze directly. "So I cheated."

The admission hung in the air like a physical thing. Murphy's expression didn't change, but Hazel saw his hands tighten slightly where they rested on his knees.

"The research data?" he asked.

"Falsified. Not all of it—the methodology was sound, the theory solid. But the results didn't support my hypothesis. Three months of work and the data said I was wrong. So I... adjusted things. Made the numbers fit what I needed them to show."

"How extensively?"

"Maybe thirty percent. Enough to transform failure into success. I told myself it didn't matter, that the theory was correct even if this particular experiment hadn't proved it. I just needed this one win."

A child's laughter echoed from the playground area, jarring against the heavy conversation. The swans continued their circuits, unimpressed by human drama.

"But Zoe found out," Hazel said.

Maeve's laugh was hollow. "Of course she did. She probably spotted the falsifications in thirty seconds. Perfect pattern recognition to go with everything else perfect about her."

"Did she confront you about it?"

Maeve's hands clenched in her lap. The swans had drifted closer to their side of the pond, elegant necks curved in question marks.

She watched them for a long moment, seeming to wrestle with something.

"Yes," she said finally, the word barely audible.

"When?" Hazel kept her voice carefully neutral.

"Yesterday." Maeve's voice had gone flat, careful. "After the lectures."

Hazel exchanged a quick glance with Murphy. His expression remained neutral, but she could see the sharpening of attention in his eyes.

"And what happened during that confrontation?" Hazel kept her voice carefully neutral.

Maeve's silence stretched out, heavy with unspoken truths. When she finally looked up, her eyes were bright with fresh tears.

"That's what I need to tell you," she whispered. "What happened in the bathroom."

42

After the Lectures

Zoe O'Brien approached Maeve's seat with the confidence of someone who'd never lost at anything. Students were still filing out of Professor Byrne's lecture hall, chattering about the surprise quiz. Maeve was shoving her textbooks into her bag when Zoe's shadow fell across her notes.

"We need to talk."

Maeve's hands stilled on her biochemistry textbook. They hadn't spoken directly since the library incident—just careful avoidance, using other students as intermediaries when group work demanded it. Whatever Zoe wanted now, it wouldn't be pleasant.

"I'm busy." Maeve zipped her bag with more force than necessary.

"This won't take long." Zoe's voice carried that particular tone she used when answering Murphy's questions—absolute certainty wrapped in false politeness. "I know what you did with your data. Your results are fake."

The words hit Maeve like ice water. Her fingers fumbled with the bag's zipper, suddenly clumsy. "I don't know what you're talking about."

"Of course you do." Zoe shifted her weight, blocking Maeve's escape route. "We should discuss this somewhere private."

"Leave me alone." Maeve stood, clutching her bag like a shield. "I need to use the bathroom."

"Perfect. The one on the ground floor." Zoe's smile was sharp as broken glass. "Barely anyone uses it. Nice and private for our conversation."

Every instinct screamed at Maeve to run. Push past Zoe, flee the building, never look back. But if Zoe really had found something, running would only delay the inevitable. And how could she have accessed the research data anyway? It was all on Maeve's laptop, password protected, backed up only to—

The flash drive.

"How did you get access to my project?" The question came out steadier than Maeve felt.

"Remember Saturday at the bookstore? When we were all getting our textbooks?" Zoe's expression shifted to something almost sympathetic. Almost. "A flash drive fell from your bag when you were digging for your wallet. I picked it up, was going to return it right away, but..." She shrugged. "Curiosity got the better of me."

Saturday. Two days ago. The Trinity bookstore, crowded with students grabbing required texts for the new term. Maeve remembered fumbling with her overstuffed bag, trying to find her wallet while juggling three heavy textbooks. Things had spilled out—pens, her phone, probably the drive too.

"I put it back in your bag this morning," Zoe continued. "During the break between lectures. You left it on your seat when you went to get coffee. Check if you don't believe me. Silver SanDisk, 32 gigs, little scratch on the corner where the keyring attaches."

Maeve's hands shook as she unzipped the front pocket of her bag. There it was, exactly as Zoe described. The scratch she'd made herself, trying to attach it to her keys six months ago. Her stomach dropped somewhere around her knees.

"Fine." The word tasted like ash. "Let's talk."

They walked to the ground floor in silence, other students flowing past in both directions, absorbed in their own concerns. The bathroom was exactly as Zoe had said—empty, forgotten, tucked away in a corner where foot traffic rarely ventured.

Zoe checked the stalls—all empty—then turned to face Maeve. She pulled out her phone, swiping to a folder labeled with yesterday's date.

"Your methodology is solid." She sounded like a professor grading papers. "The theoretical framework? Brilliant, actually. Better than mine in some ways. But the results..." She turned the phone screen toward Maeve. "Thirty percent of your data points are statistically impossible. The p-values are too perfect. And this graph?" She swiped to another image. "The error bars are identical across all conditions. That never happens with actual data."

Each word was another nail in Maeve's academic coffin. She stared at the phone screen, seeing months of work reduced to evidence of fraud. All those twelve-hour days analyzing data, the exhaustion, the pressure—ending here in a bathroom that smelled of industrial cleaner and broken dreams.

"What do you want?" Maeve's voice came out smaller than intended.

"Drop out of the grant competition." Zoe tucked the phone back in her pocket. "Withdraw your application today. Say you need more time to refine your research, family obligations, whatever excuse works. But you're done competing for the Brennan-Walsh Fellowship."

"I can't just drop out. I've worked for months on this project—"

"Apparently not hard enough." Zoe's laugh was like fingernails on glass. "Since you had to fake your results to make it work."

The casual cruelty of it made Maeve's chest tight. As if the hours didn't count because desperation had driven her to falsify the final pieces. As if the theory being sound meant nothing because the experiment hadn't cooperated.

"You just admitted my framework was brilliant." Maeve hated how her voice cracked. "Better than yours."

"It is." Zoe stepped closer, close enough that Maeve could smell her perfume—something expensive and subtle. "Which makes this even more pathetic. You had real potential, Maeve. You just weren't quite good enough to execute it. And rather than accept that, you cheated."

"You don't understand the pressure—"

"Drop out today." Zoe's voice went low, dangerous. "Or I email everything to the grant committee. And Murphy. And the academic board. Your choice."

The bathroom walls seemed to close in. Both options led to disaster. Drop out, and face her parents' disappointment, their questions, the weight of wasted money and time. Stay in, and Zoe would destroy her—not just the grant, but her entire academic future. Research fraud would follow her forever, closing doors before she could even knock.

Years of pressure compressed into this moment. Her father's voice echoed in her memory: *"Second place isn't good enough."* Her mother's quiet sacrifices. The loans, the double shifts, the faith that their daughter would make it all worthwhile.

And here stood Zoe O'Brien, who'd never wanted for anything, who absorbed knowledge like breathing, who won without trying. Everything Maeve had scraped and fought for, Zoe possessed naturally. Now she wanted to take away even Maeve's desperate attempt to compete.

"Well?" Zoe moved even closer, barely a foot between them now. "What's it going to be?"

Maeve could see her own reflection in Zoe's eyes—pale, terrified, cornered. This close, she could see the small scar on Zoe's left eyebrow, the way her lipstick had worn off except at the corners. Human details that somehow made it worse.

"I need time to think—"

"I'm being generous giving you until end of day." Zoe's breath was warm against Maeve's face. "But then, I've always been better than you at everything. Even mercy."

The words were whispered, almost intimate. The final insult delivered with surgical precision.

Something snapped inside Maeve. All the pressure, the fear, the constant shadow of coming second—it condensed into her hands, into movement she didn't consciously decide. She shoved Zoe hard, both palms against her shoulders, putting all her frustration into the push.

Zoe hadn't expected it. Why would she? She was Zoe O'Brien, untouchable, always in control. She stumbled backward, arms windmilling for balance that wouldn't come. Her eyes went wide—surprise more than fear, like a calculation error she couldn't quite process.

The back of Zoe's head connected with the porcelain sink with a sound like a dropped melon. Dull. Final. She crumpled to the floor in a graceless heap, blonde hair fanning across the white tiles.

For three heartbeats, Maeve stood frozen. This wasn't real. Couldn't be real. Any second now, Zoe would sit up, furious but fine. Any second.

"Zoe?" Maeve dropped to her knees beside the still form. "Oh God, are you okay? I didn't mean—"

Blood. Spreading beneath Zoe's head like spilled wine, dark against the white tiles. Too much blood. The smell of it—copper and wrongness—made Maeve's stomach heave.

She reached out with shaking hands, touched Zoe's shoulder. No response. The brilliant eyes that had dissected Maeve's fraud stared at nothing, already going glassy.

Footsteps echoed in the hallway outside. Someone humming off-key, getting closer.

Maeve's body moved without her permission. She scrambled to her feet, bag clutched against her chest, and bolted for the other exit. The one that led to the back stairwell, rarely used, perfect for escape.

The bathroom door opened behind her. A pause. Then Aisling Grant's scream split the air, high and horrified, the sound that would echo in Maeve's nightmares for the rest of her life.

But Maeve was already gone, taking the stairs two at a time, fleeing from what she'd done. From Zoe O'Brien's last whispered words and the wet crack of skull meeting porcelain. From the knowledge that she'd finally beaten Zoe at something.

She'd won the worst competition of all.

43

Professor Murphy listened to Maeve's confession with the detached part of his mind that had carried him through forty years of teaching—the part that could grade papers while his personal life crumbled, that could explain enzyme kinetics through any crisis. But underneath that professional distance, something fundamental shifted.

A push. That's all it had taken. One moment of snapped control, hands moving faster than thought, and Zoe O'Brien's brilliant mind was reduced to tissue and electrical impulses fading on a bathroom floor. The mundane horror of it made his chest tight.

"I didn't mean to kill her." Maeve's voice was barely audible over the pond's gentle lapping. "It was an accident. The angle, the force—everything went wrong. If things had been just slightly different, she'd be alive. Just bruised maybe, but alive."

The swans had given up their circuits, settling near the pond's edge to preen. One extended its neck, bill working methodically through white feathers. Such simple creatures, swans. No capacity for lies or fraud or the terrible arithmetic of academic pressure.

"You have to believe me." Maeve turned to him, eyes red-rimmed and desperate. "Yesterday, after—I went home and sat in my room and couldn't process it. Kept thinking I'd imagined the whole thing. That I'd wake up and it would be Monday again, before any of this happened."

Murphy had seen this before, though never quite so dramatically. The way pressure could warp judgment, make good students do terrible things. Hadn't he watched dozens of them crack over the decades? Plagiarism, sabotage, nervous breakdowns. But never murder. Never this.

"But this morning it all came back." Maeve wiped her nose with her sleeve, a childish gesture that made her seem even younger. "The sound her head made. The blood. Aisling screaming. I couldn't—I had to tell someone."

Hazel shifted on the bench, and Murphy caught her expression. Sympathy mixed with something harder. She'd solved murders in Paris and Rome, had faced killers who planned their crimes with cold precision. This—a young woman overwhelmed by pressure, lashing out in a moment of panic—was different but no less tragic.

"Am I going to prison?" Maeve's question came out small, frightened. "My parents—God, they'll disown me. All that money, all those sacrifices, and their daughter's a murderer."

Murphy found himself thinking of Zoe's files, those clinical observations of her classmates. She'd documented Maeve's breaking point with scientific precision but hadn't accounted for one variable: human unpredictability. In her behavioral studies, she'd forgotten that her subjects weren't just data points. They were people, capable of snapping when pushed too far.

"Listen to me carefully." He kept his voice steady, professorial. "What you've described sounds like manslaughter, not murder. You didn't plan this, didn't intend for Zoe to die. With proper legal representation, that distinction matters."

"We don't have money for lawyers." Fresh tears started down Maeve's cheeks. "We can barely afford my education."

"There are options. Legal aid, pro bono work. But first, you need to go to the Gardaí. Today. Now. Tell them exactly what you've told us." He paused, choosing his words carefully. "The fact that you're coming forward voluntarily, that you're showing genuine remorse—it will be taken into consideration."

Maeve nodded miserably, looking younger than her twenty years. Just a scared girl who'd made one terrible decision that couldn't be undone. Murphy felt the weight of it—two brilliant students, both flawed in their own ways, one dead and one facing prison. What a waste.

"We'll go with you," Hazel offered, but Murphy shook his head slightly.

"Best if Miss Delaney and I handle this." He gave Hazel a meaningful look. "No need to complicate matters with... international involvement. I believe you've had enough of that in Rome and Paris?"

Relief flickered across Hazel's face. She understood—her role as amateur detective needed to stay in the shadows. The Gardaí would have questions enough without learning about the American tourist who'd somehow helped solve three deaths across Europe.

They stood, Maeve moving like someone underwater. Murphy touched her shoulder gently, and she flinched.

"I'll stay with you through the process," he promised. "You're still my student. That means something."

She managed a weak smile that broke his heart a little. How many times had he stood at the front of lecture halls, watching these young minds absorb knowledge, never thinking one day he'd be walking one to confess to killing another?

As they left the park, Maeve trailing beside him like a lost child, Murphy found himself thinking about coincidences. Thomas and Olivia's daughter, appearing in his life after twenty-three years. A death in his own program, just as Hazel arrived. The past and present colliding in ways that defied probability.

He'd never expected to meet Hazel Chase, had assumed that chapter of his life—his connection to Thomas and Olivia—was closed forever. But here she was, helping him understand how one of his students had killed another. Life could be strange and cruel and surprising all at once.

The Gardaí station loomed ahead, all modern glass and institutional authority. Maeve stopped walking, staring at it like it might swallow her whole.

"I can't," she whispered.

"You can." Murphy kept his voice firm but kind. "You've done the hardest part—admitting what happened. The rest is just process."

She took a shaky breath, squared her shoulders, and walked through the station doors. Murphy followed, already composing the phone calls he'd need to make. Legal aid. The university administration. Maeve's parents, though that conversation could wait until she'd given her statement.

Behind them, Dublin carried on—tourists taking photos, students heading to afternoon lectures, the ordinary business of a city that didn't know or care that one young woman's life had just changed forever. Murphy envied them their ignorance. Some knowledge, once gained, sat heavy in your chest forever.

Like knowing that brilliance and pressure and one moment of violence could destroy two futures at once.

44

The evening sun painted Dublin's buildings in shades of gold and amber, the kind of light that made even concrete look romantic. Hazel sat on her B&B bed, still processing everything Maeve had confessed. The clinical way Zoe had documented her classmates. The desperate falsification of data. That final push born of pressure and panic.

Her phone buzzed. Emily calling.

"Please tell me you're free tonight," Emily said without preamble. "Patrick and I are dying to know what happened. The whole campus is buzzing about Maeve going to the Gardaí station with Professor Murphy."

Hazel had been planning to spend the evening scrolling through her phone, maybe grabbing takeaway from that Thai place she'd spotted. But Emily's eagerness was hard to resist, and honestly, talking through the case might help her process it.

"Where should we meet?"

"Trinity entrance? We can take a walk along the river."

Twenty minutes later, Hazel stood at Trinity's gates watching students stream past. Evening lectures, late library sessions, or just heading to pubs—the rhythm of university life continuing despite yesterday's tragedy. She spotted Patrick and Emily approaching together, their familiar figures easy to pick out from the crowd.

"Right," Patrick said by way of greeting. "Spill everything. The rumors are completely mad—everything from Maeve being a serial killer to Zoe faking her own death."

"Definitely not a serial killer." Hazel fell into step beside them as they headed toward the river. "Just a desperate student who made one terrible decision."

They walked along the Liffey, the water reflecting the sunset in rippling fragments. Georgian buildings lined the riverbank, their brick facades softened by centuries of Irish weather. Hazel told them about the investigation and how it led to Maeve's confession, keeping Darragh's role in the photo incident to herself as promised.

"So it really was just an accident?" Emily sounded almost disappointed. "After all that drama with affairs and rivalries?"

"Manslaughter, technically. The academic rivalry created the pressure, but the actual death?" Hazel shrugged. "Wrong place, wrong angle, wrong moment."

They passed a crowded pub, music and laughter spilling onto the street. A hen party stumbled past, the bride-to-be wearing a veil made of toilet paper and a sash declaring her "Dublin's Drunkest Bride."

"The photo thing though," Patrick said, lowering his voice. "We still haven't figured out who sent it."

"Neither have I," Hazel said, keeping her voice neutral. "Whoever it is, they're keeping quiet."

Emily sighed. "Everyone from the camping trip swears they were asleep when the photo was taken. No one admits to seeing anything. It's like the picture took itself."

"Maybe someone wants to stay anonymous," Hazel suggested.

"Can't blame them," Patrick agreed. "Cian's been pretty aggressive about tracking down the photographer. Smart to stay quiet."

They turned onto the quays, heading toward the modern section of Dublin where glass and steel reached skyward. The Samuel Beckett Bridge appeared ahead, its distinctive harp shape spanning the Liffey. As twilight deepened, LED lights along the cables shifted from blue to purple to green, the bridge becoming a piece of kinetic art against the darkening sky. The contrast with the older parts of the city was jarring—centuries colliding in architectural form.

"How's Aisling taking it?" Hazel asked.

"About as well as you'd expect," Emily said. "She cornered us before the afternoon lectures, absolutely raging. 'How could you know about the affair and not tell me? What kind of friends are you?' That sort of thing."

"She'll get over it," Patrick said, but he didn't sound convinced. "Eventually. Maybe. Probably not, actually."

"She won't forget the affair," Emily agreed. "There's no going back from that. But she might forgive us for keeping quiet. Especially since Cian's already moving on."

"Already?"

"Saw him chatting up some first-year outside the Biomed," Patrick confirmed. "Had his whole routine going—the lean against the wall, the crooked smile, the way he kept finding excuses to touch her arm while they talked."

"Aisling deserves better," Emily said firmly. "Someone who actually appreciates her."

They'd reached the convention center, its tilted glass cylinder glowing from within. The area felt like a different city entirely—tech company headquarters and expensive apartments, workers streaming out of offices toward the Liffey's edge.

"Question for you," Emily said as they paused to admire the bridge. "Aisling said you were Murphy's research assistant. Darragh insists you're a private investigator from America. But you told us you were just here to learn about your parents. So which is it?"

Hazel found herself smiling. "All true, in a way. I helped Murphy research what happened—assistant work. I investigated the death—detective work. And I am here about my parents—the personal part."

"But primarily?" Patrick pressed.

"Primarily, I'm just a baker from California."

The words sat strangely in her mouth. Was that still true? After three cities, three deaths, three investigations, could she still claim to be just a baker? The skills she'd developed—reading people, following leads, pushing for truth—they were becoming as much a part of her as knowing the perfect proofing time for sourdough.

They talked until full darkness fell, the city lights reflecting in the river like fallen stars. When they finally parted ways—Emily and Patrick heading back to student housing, Hazel to her B&B—she felt the weight of transition. Her Dublin investigation was over. Zoe's killer had confessed. Time to move on.

But first, a few days to breathe.

45

The next morning, Hazel woke with a decision: no more death for at least forty-eight hours. She was in Dublin, damn it, and she was going to be a tourist if it killed her. Though given her track record, she immediately regretted that particular phrase.

She spent the day hitting every cliché on the list. The Guinness Storehouse, where she learned seven floors' worth of beer facts and pretended the view from the Gravity Bar made the overpriced ticket worthwhile. Dublin Castle in the afternoon, wandering through state apartments and medieval undercrofts, trying to imagine centuries of power plays within these walls.

That evening, she called Janet from her room, feet aching from walking.

"Please tell me you're calling from the airport," Janet said immediately. "Heading home where people don't regularly die around you."

"The investigation's closed. Maeve confessed."

"Maeve? Which one was—never mind, doesn't matter. What matters is you coming home before someone else inconveniently dies in your vicinity."

"I'm being careful. Taking a few days to just be a tourist. Museums, historical sites, overpriced gift shops. Very safe, very boring."

"You said Rome would be safe too. Then five people tried to kill you."

"Technically only two were seriously trying. The others were just going along with—you know what, not important." Hazel picked at a loose thread on the duvet. "I'm flying to Amsterdam on Saturday."

The silence stretched long enough that Hazel checked her phone to make sure the call hadn't dropped.

"Janet?"

"I'm practicing my surprised face for when you call me about the Amsterdam murder. Want to sound convincing."

"There won't be an Amsterdam murder."

"Sure. And I'll be dating someone emotionally available by Christmas."

After they hung up, Hazel called Mike. It felt natural now, like the past year of silence had been a bad dream. He answered on the second ring, keyboard clicking in the background.

"Hey," she said. "Thought I'd update you. The case is closed—turned out to be a student who killed Zoe in an argument over falsified research data."

"I knew it had to be something like that. Academic pressure makes people crazy." Keys clicked faster. "So no more murders to report?"

"Not yet. I'm being very careful."

"You've been there what, three days now?"

"Four actually. And the murder happened on day two, thank you very much. I'm improving."

He laughed, and the sound made something in her chest loosen. "How's Dublin?"

She told him about her day, the tourist traps and genuine moments of connection with history. He shared stories from the shop—Mrs. Chen had brought in a laptop filled with so much cat hair he'd needed an actual vacuum to clean it, and someone had tried to pay for virus removal with homemade jam.

"Strawberry, at least?"

"Apricot. I'm allergic to apricots."

"The universe has a weird sense of humor."

A door chimed in the background, followed by a female voice calling out, "Mike? You ready?"

"Oh, hey—" Mike's voice shifted, suddenly hurried. "That's Grace. We're grabbing lunch. I should go."

"Sure, of course." The words came out too fast. "Talk later."

"Yeah, I'll—"

But he'd already hung up. Hazel set the phone down slowly, staring at the ceiling. She shouldn't care that Grace and Mike were having lunch together. She and Mike used to grab lunch all the time—quick burritos between his repair jobs, sandwiches eaten while he explained why her laptop was making weird noises. Now Grace had taken her place in that routine. Which was fine. Completely fine.

The next two days passed in determined tourism. She took Mrs. O'Neill's advice and caught the DART to Howth, spending hours walking the cliff path while wind tried to blow her into the Irish Sea. The village was postcard perfect—fishing boats bobbing in the harbor, seafood restaurants promising the catch of the day, houses climbing the hillside in colorful tiers. She ate fish and chips on a bench, watching seals play in the harbor, and didn't think about murder at all.

The National Museum occupied most of another day. She wandered through exhibitions of Viking artifacts and ancient gold, reading every placard like there'd be a test later. A school group swarmed past, their teacher trying vainly to stop them from touching things. One boy pressed his nose against a display case, leaving a perfect smudge, and Hazel found herself smiling.

The morning of her flight to Amsterdam, her phone rang. Professor Murphy.

"I hope I'm not calling too early," he said. "But Riona and I were hoping to see you before you leave. She's had some time to process things since the funeral, and she specifically asked if we could all meet."

"Of course. Where?"

"Trinity campus, if that works? Where this all started seems appropriate for goodbye."

Forty minutes later, Hazel walked through Trinity's gates one last time. The campus was quieter than usual—Saturday morning meant fewer students—and she found Murphy and Riona waiting by the Campanile.

Riona looked better than the last time Hazel had seen her. Still grieving, always grieving, but the raw edges had softened slightly. She'd styled her hair, applied light makeup. Small steps toward normalcy.

"Hazel." Riona took both her hands, squeezing gently. "I wanted to thank you properly. For everything you did."

"I just asked questions."

"You found the truth. That matters more than you know." They started walking, no particular destination. "Your parents would have been proud. Olivia especially—she always loved puzzles."

The casual mention of her mother's personality hit unexpectedly hard. These small details—loves puzzles, brilliant smile, argumentative with Thomas about enzyme kinetics—built a picture of a real person, not just the tragic figure in Hazel's imagination.

"I'm sorry we couldn't meet under better circumstances," Hazel said.

"So am I." Riona's smile was sad but genuine. "Though knowing Olivia and Thomas, they would have found meaning in this. Their daughter, here in Dublin, trying to understand what happened to mine. The universe has a cruel sense of timing sometimes."

They passed a group of students deep in debate about James Joyce, hands gesturing wildly as they dissected symbolism and meaning. Normal university life, continuing despite everything.

"Can I ask you something?" Hazel chose her words carefully. "About forgiveness?"

Riona's expression didn't change, but something shifted in her posture. "About Maeve."

"Can you forgive her? Ever?"

They walked in silence past the rugby pitch, where someone was already practicing despite the early hour. The sound of boot hitting ball echoed across the grass.

"I understand why she did it," Riona said finally. "The pressure, the moment of anger, the terrible accident of angle and gravity. Intellectually, I can process all of that. But forgiveness?" She shook her head. "She took my only child. My brilliant, difficult, complicated daughter. How do you forgive that?"

"I don't know."

"No. I don't suppose anyone does until they're faced with it." Riona turned to study her. "Let me ask you something in return. If you discovered your parents' death wasn't an accident—if someone had deliberately caused that car crash—could you forgive them?"

Hazel's steps faltered. She glanced at Murphy, who cleared his throat.

"I told Riona about Amsterdam," he explained. "About your plans to investigate Haldrek Pharmaceuticals. It seemed relevant, given everything."

"I couldn't forgive," Hazel said honestly. "Even understanding why, even with explanations and reasons—no. Some things cut too deep."

"Then you understand my position with Maeve." Riona's voice was steady but sad. "Though I do hope she gets fair treatment. She's young, and one terrible moment shouldn't define an entire life. Even if it ended one."

They'd circled back toward the entrance, their walk coming to a natural end. The morning was warming up, September sun fighting through clouds.

"About Amsterdam," Riona said suddenly. "Cornelius told me about the men who came asking questions after your parents died. They came to me too."

"They did?"

"Two of them, claiming to be from Haldrek's legal department. Very polite, very persistent. Wanted to know if Thomas or Olivia had sent me anything, left anything in my care. When I said no, they got... less polite."

"They threatened you?"

"Suggested that memory could be a funny thing. That sometimes people remembered things wrong, and that could be dangerous." Riona's jaw tightened. "I was young, scared, had just lost two former classmates. I convinced myself it was grief making me paranoid. But looking back..."

"You think my parents were murdered."

"I think they got involved in something that powerful people wanted stopped. And I think you should be very careful in Amsterdam." She touched Hazel's arm. "I couldn't protect Zoe from an angry classmate. But maybe I can warn you about walking into something larger than you realize."

Murphy nodded agreement. "The fact that Haldrek is still operating, still successful, suggests they survived whatever your parents might have discovered. Companies don't survive scandals without protecting themselves. Aggressively."

"I have to know." Hazel heard the stubbornness in her own voice, Bridget's influence maybe. Or maybe just her own need for answers overriding common sense. "Twenty-three years of questions, and I'm this close. If someone killed them, if there's evidence in Amsterdam, I need to find it."

"Even if those same people come after you?" Riona asked.

"Even then."

They stood at Trinity's gates, Dublin flowing past in its morning rhythm. Somewhere in this city, Maeve Delaney was probably meeting with lawyers, preparing a defense for pushing too hard at the wrong moment. Somewhere else, Aisling Grant was learning to rebuild after betrayal. Life moving forward, messy and complicated and unavoidable.

"Be careful," Murphy said simply. "Whatever you find in Amsterdam, whatever truth waits there—be very careful. And remember, you have my number if you need anything."

Hazel promised she would, knowing even as she said it that careful was a relative term. She'd been careful in Paris and Rome too, and look how that had turned out.

But Amsterdam was waiting, and with it, the possibility of finally understanding what had really happened to Thomas and Olivia Chase. Whether Haldrek Pharmaceuticals had silenced them for what they'd discovered. Whether their car crash had been orchestrated by someone protecting corporate secrets.

The possibility that someone in Amsterdam had been getting away with murder for twenty-three years.

Time to change that.

The End
… of the third book in the series

Author's Note

Thank you so much for reading this book! I hope you had fun following Hazel through the rainy streets of Dublin as she solved yet another mystery.

Like in *Murder in Rome*, I've woven in something from my own Dublin experience. That confusing entrance to Dublin Pearse station? I spent ages looking for it too, just like Hazel! And while I may have been a bit harsh on Dublin's weather in this book (sorry, Dublin!), the city is absolutely worth visiting. The truth is, you just need a bit of Irish luck to time your visit right—you actually can catch some lovely sunshine between the showers.

This book wraps up the first arc of the series, where we've been slowly piecing together Hazel's parents' university past. As you've probably guessed by now, the next book in Amsterdam will kick off a new arc focused on Haldrek Pharmaceuticals—and I have a feeling things are about to get a lot more dangerous for our amateur detective.

If you enjoyed the book, I'd really appreciate it if you could leave a review on Amazon or Goodreads—or both, if you're up for it. I genuinely read every single one, and your feedback means the world to me.

Want to be the first to know about new releases and updates? Sign up for my newsletter, and as a thank you, you'll receive a FREE exclusive short story: *Takedown in Fillmore.* It reveals how Hazel went from the worst student in her self-defense class to defeating her longtime rival—a fun glimpse into her teenage years in Fillmore that I wrote just for my newsletter subscribers.

ArthurPearce.com/Newsletter

Thanks again for coming along on this journey with Hazel and me. See you in the next city!

Hazel's Story Continues

What deadly secrets await at Haldrek Pharmaceuticals?
Find out in *Murder in Amsterdam*!

Also by Arthur Pearce

Jim and Ginger Cozy Mysteries
A retired librarian and his cat solve mysteries in a coastal town

Printed in Dunstable, United Kingdom